3 8012

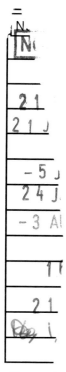

=
N

N

2 1
2 1 J

- 5 J
2 4 J.
- 3 A

1

2 1

Please l
or chang

Too Fast to Die

Charron, a notorious and villainous renegade, ordered his henchmen to rob the Mexican church of Santa Catarina of its reputedly large hoard of treasure by excavating under the building. But disaster struck and the church collapsed leaving eight of the nine thieves dead. As luck would have it Charron was the only one to escape.

Then Chance Stellarman entered the frame. His deadly mission was to hunt down the renegade who had built a new life for himself. But could Chance nail the killer and still live to tell the tale?

Here is a gripping story with no holds barred.

Too Fast to Die

Dempsey Clay

A Black Horse Western

ROBERT HALE · LONDON

ISBN 978-0-7090-8374-0

Robert Hale Limited
Clerkenwell House
Clerkenwell Green
London EC1R 0HT

Typeset by
Derek Doyle & Associates, Shaw Heath
Printed and bound in Great Britain by
Antony Rowe Limited, Wiltshire

CHAPTER 1

WHERE CHARRON RIDES

Even Virgil the giant *renegado* paled beneath the brim of his dusty sombrero when he realized what Charron expected of him – what indeed the leader wanted from all four of them.

He plainly wanted them to enter the crumbling church of Santa Catarina in search of the precious icons rumoured to have been secreted away in the subterranean vaults when the Rio Magdalena had finally undercut this long abandoned place of worship. Wished them to go in there now at a time when the brawling mountain stream was running a-banker again? Surely he spoke in jest?

He was forgetting for the moment that the pistolero standing before him in the slanting after-noon sunlight never joked when dealing with important matters, such as money or authority.

'Virgil, Virgil,' the handsome killer said with a flashing, phony smile, resting a hand on the big man's shoulder. 'Tell me honestly, do I look as though I jest?'

'Well, perhaps not, *amigo*, but surely—'

The hand dropped away sharply.

'Then why are you still here?' Charron rapped. He gestured brusquely at the others. 'Why are you all still standing about like fools when I have wasted so much time in bringing you here to reveal my great secret? Well, who answers? Romero, Santini, Vaca . . . or perhaps you, little Savino? Come, come, Charron only wishes to hear what you are thinking. You do not fear I might be angered to suddenly discover my brave *bandidos* might be afraid of a few cracks in the walls or a little water in the vaults, do you?'

They were more than afraid; they were scared stiff. For several violent weeks spent in the company of the outlaw known famously in many a Mexican bullring simply as 'The Matador', had taught them one vital primary lesson. This was, that whenever he might be crossed, Charron's response could be frightening enough to scare a stone saint, such as the one gazing placidly down upon them from the tilting roof of the sacristy at that moment.

'Well, perhaps we were feeling a little weary from the riding is all, *companero*,' Balthazar placated hastily, and turned briskly to his henchmen. 'I do believe we now are ready to do . . . ahh . . . whatever it is that must be done, eh my brave *muchachas*?'

Who would disagree with this with Charron standing there smiling with the eyes of a tiger?

It went quickly from there. Grabbing up the digging implements they'd secured in the tiny village close by, and with giant Virgil leading the way, the outlaws entered the church to stare about wide-eyed at the fading wall-paintings and tryptiches of ancient saints and martyrs which seemed to gaze back at them with saddened eyes for the sacrileges they were about to commit.

The intruders' way led through several crumbling chambers littered with smashed caskets, chunks of fallen masonry and water-rotted timbers.

It was the river finally undercutting the foundations of the church which had eventually rendered it too dangerous for use by the faithful. From time to time since the closure, only reckless thieves had ventured here, drawn by tales of vast treasures squirrelled away in the lower chambers by the old monks and priests. Some had survived the experience with maybe a few centavos' worth of brass icons and such to show for the risks they ran. But they were the lucky ones. With the brawling Rio Magdalena now surging against the northern walls of the church of Santa Catarina itself, total collapse had been threatening for months, and surely robbers had perished here already to convince all but the insane that the hunt really was not worth the danger.

And until today, that had been the case for well over a month during which time the citizens of Agua Prieta had awakened every morning fully expecting to find the centuries-old place of worship washed away in the torrent.

If Charron had any fears, he gave no sign. His henchmen were hardly surprised. It was agreed amongst them that a man ready and willing to face a man with a gun, or – even more chillingly – to step into a bullring on some lazy Sabbath afternoon and face a giant fighting bull of the province, armed with nothing more than a cape and an itty-bitty sword, was surely very unlikely to be spooked by creaking walls, falling plaster and the deep subterranean groaning where the river was eating away at the building's foundations.

He led them unhesitatingly down several flights of stone steps and on through echoing, cobwebbed chambers to eventually reach the crypt where rested several good men of God and more than a few who had no more hope of reaching Paradise than Charron himself, which meant no single glimmer of hope at all.

'Far enough.' Charron's voice echoed hollowly in the cold crypt. 'Martinez, you stand watch from the priests' confessionals up top. If you leave for any reason, I will shoot your companeros first, then you. Now get out.'

With a helpless glance over his shoulder at his henchmen, gaunt Martinez quit that ghostly chamber. On his way back towards the stronger light, he passed beneath an archway supported by freshly hewn timbers, a safety feature erected by earlier tomb-robbers following a masonry fall which crushed to death five of their party.

The corpses had been dumped in a confessional and now stunk like hell.

Passing a statue of the virgin, the renegade wished momentarily that he had the faith to believe that a prayer to the divine lady might result in her smiting Charron down with a lightning bolt, leaving the rest of them free to bolt back to the fastnesses of the mountains where they might return to the far simpler business of murdering and robbing the poor once again, and the devil take all holy treasures.

Charron listened to the man's steps fade away then turned his attention to a small pile of gold ornaments, which thus far was all his diggers had managed to prise from beneath the rubble.

Brushing the pieces to the floor with a muttered curse, he whirled to see them all staring fearfully over their shoulders at him. He stamped a booted foot and they jumped back into action again, dirt, rock and rubble flying from their short-handled shovels.

In sequence on their terror scale, the outlaws placed Charron first, followed by the river and finally the groaning and creaking structure overhead. Some even had enough fear left over to fret about Bester and the chance he might hear what was happening here and possibly return to defend what he believed to be his by right.

Charron knew little of the gringo outlaw who'd spent a perilous month ransacking the church before being driven off by a Rurale patrol which happened by. But Hunch Bester, fatally infected by the treasure bug, had not run too far. Indeed he had been close enough to eventually get wind of Charron and his interest in the church. Spurred by this, he had just spent half a day leading his killers down out of the towering Zantigo Mountains to finally clatter into the village of Agua Prieta which lay beyond the wooded hill, which obscured that poor place from sight of the river.

Until the moment he saw for himself that the supposed treasures of the church of Santa Catarina, which he now regarded as his by right of might, appeared to be in imminent danger, the New Mexican outlaw had maintained a disciplined calm in the face of adversity. Yet discipline was just a memory when he first heard the name 'Charron', while total fury overtook him the moment he peered from cover to actually sight the tethered outlaw horses and a big-nosed Martinez leaning upon his long rifle half-visible through a gaping hole in the wall of the cloister.

'Thieving, sacrilegious scum!' he snarled, unmindful of his hypocrisy.

Next moment he was moving fast, fearful that even a moment's delay might have caused him to remember all the bloody tales he'd heard about the Matador, and maybe take to his heels instead.

Hunch Bester fiercely wanted to believe the church contained great riches, and now he was back he found himself able to blank his mind to all the ominous creakings and groanings he'd experienced here before, which had finally forced him to quit in simple funk.

Now his mind-set would not budge beyond the point where he truly believed that, should any man get to unearth the fabled treasures of the holy church of Santa Catarina, it would be Hunch Bester.

The hellions moved in afoot, five stealthy shapes with guns reflecting the flickering light of the brand Martinez had just lighted inside when the sun went down.

Some eighty metres farther along the subterranean corridors from the newcomers' position, a lithe figure clad in black and a tip-tilted sombrero, stood before a canting altar scowling down at his workers. They were sweating and groaning with exhaustion as any man might. Yet until now their combined labors had produced nothing more than several more altar pieces of little value. And now a single wooden crucifix.

Wood!

Charron hurled the cross viciously at Savino, who ducked. The piece struck a stanchion and ricocheted off to catch Romero a glancing blow to the face. The Coyotero hard man grabbed at his cheek, saw the blood on his fingers – and promptly lost his temper.

He snatched at his .45, but froze.

'Ladies first, Romero – after you.'

Charron stood with arms folded flashing a taunting smile, challenging the man to draw. While every instinct warned him to caution, Romero was suddenly too angry to heed reason. Their original quest for the treasure had been all Charron's idea, and he'd always reckoned it a highly reckless and dangerous one. Their labour and the dangers encountered here before would turn a strong man gray. He'd then fought against the leader's decision to return, and had lost.

Right now he was more scared of this creaking tomb of a place and the very real prospect of being buried alive than of any *pistolero* who ever walked.

Even in that hanging moment when the angry outlaw realized that to draw would be to die, Romero was angry and frightened enough to defy the odds and come clear anyway.

He might well have done so but for the sound that emanated from the recessed wall cupboard which Vaca had been struggling to prise open over several minutes.

The man had wedged a jemmy between cupboard and corner, when he'd heard the faint clunk of sound. But it was only when he released the pressure of the jemmy that something rattled within. Something metallic.

Ignoring Romero as though he no longer existed, Charron sprang across the crypt in one bound, seized the cupboard handle and reefed it violently open, seemingly without effort.

A goblet fashioned from solid gold thudded to the littered floor of the chamber at his feet.

The cupboard was otherwise empty. But the goblet alone was more than sufficient to refire the enthusiasm of every outlaw, even Romero, who promptly led the way downwards side by side with Charron.

So there really was treasure to be found in this place after all!

Martinez was dreaming of wealth beyond imagining when he should have been as vividly alert at his look-out post as a stud pig at a knackering.

It was the hard-bitten Balthazar who got to the dreaming lookout and drove a foot-long blade into his back with as little compunction as one might stamp an ant. The brutal taking of a life occupied but seconds, resulting in five hard-bitten hellions with naked guns starting off along the first corridor they came to leading downwards.

Taut with excitement, Bester led his dog pack past a line of crumbling pews and ducked his head below a marble holy water font which now held nothing but dust.

Excited voices sounded from somewhere up ahead and below.

They found both nave and sanctuary empty of life. To the right stood a low opened door. Bester glanced upwards and saw the winding staircase that climbed to the bell towers. He heard the bell softly clanging and paused long enough to frown in puzzlement. Not a breath of wind this evening, so how come the chiming?

It was a small mystery which, no matter how seem-ingly innocuous and seemingly, should really have been investigated. There could have been many explanations including the one that the entire

13

construction may have tilted fractionally on this windless night.

Bester swung away confidently to lead the way downwards. Ancient walls were faded and peeling. Everywhere were signs of scavenging, some perpetrated by his own bunch before they were thrown one scare too many by this creaking, groaning ruin, and fled to the hills.

Above a familiar altar the marble head of a saint stared down with sorrow and calm forgiveness. Bester's lip curled in a sneer as he strode into the sacristy where rickety stairs led down to the lower chambers where some riches were supposed to be hidden.

The big man sucked in a deep breath. It was here that one heard clearly for the first time the soft rushing sounds of the river swirling restlessly against the crumbling foundations of this centuries-old place of worship.

It was the Rio Magdalena itself that had first encroached all the way across the church yard to the walls of the building after eventually sluicing away the tons and tons of soft bank formerly separating them. The day that finally happened was the day the town closed the church down, leaving it to the bats, the eternal moaning and groaning of its underpinnings, and its eventual intruders and plunderers.

Ancient fallen bricks and chunks of shattered plaster sought to impede the outlaws' progress as they followed Bester's powerful figure down towards the final chamber.

His mouth was dust dry as, gun cocked and ready in his big brown fist, the grim-jawed outlaw led them towards the light at the end of the fifty-foot corridor stretching before them.

Soon, the light from within fell across the toes of the outlaw's boots.

They stopped when they heard the voices.

'I think there is another chalice in here, Charron.'

'Then get in there and look, *stupido*!'

'This chalice is so beautiful . . . is it to be mine since it was I who found the cupboard, Charron?'

'Dream if it pleases you, *capon*. Well, is there more within?'

Bester waited until the sounds of activity resumed then peered around the stonework with infinite caution. He saw the lean, dark-garbed figure of Charron standing with his back to the entrance as four men attempted to jerk the protesting cupboard loose of its aperture, the whole scene lighted by a lantern resting upon a bench across the room.

His mouth painfully dry, Bester raised his Colt .45, and was drawing a bead on Charron's back when one of the Matador's men lost his grip on the slowly yielding cupboard and fell backwards, cannoning into his tall figure.

Bester could not believe it when he accidentally jerked the trigger. It was an involuntary action caused by the two figures falling backwards towards him. He'd had no intention of firing a gun down here where any loud noises or vibrations could set the whole uneasy structure groaning and creaking in a way that could terrify even a cold-blooded killer like Hunch Bester.

The wild bullet whipped harmlessly by Charron's shoulder. In one dazzling blur of movement, the *pistolero* whirled, palmed Colt and triggered, filling the chamber for the second time with the brutal enclosed blast of a roaring sixgun.

'No!' someone howled. 'No shooting! The whole fragging place will come down if—'

That was as far as he got as the frantic cry, along with every other noise in the underground, was swallowed by the most menacing sound this side of eternity – the great slow creaking and groaning overhead of eroded and undermined canyons of stone, earth, rock, plaster, marble and timber fighting to resist that violent intrusion of imprisoned sound and power touched off initially by one gunshot, then a dozen more as violent men who knew only guns, began shooting in one last nightmare of violent frenzy – fighting to gain the exit none would ever reach.

The ancient church of Santa Catarina tottered and shuddered, then collapsed with a roar like the end of the world.

Outside, great billows of dust were rising high above the tumbling mass of collapsing masonry that was only too quickly engulfed and extinguished by the surging waters of the Rio Magdalena foaming in through shattered walls.

The villagers who came rushing through the trees

stopped in their tracks to stare disbelievingly down upon the scene of chaos, saw only Martinez the lookout, sodden and bloodied, clawing his way upwards until eager hands hauled him out of the jaws of the maelstrom.

'*Muertos?*' an ashen-faced man cried. 'All *muertos?*'

'Yeah,' the sole survivor panted. 'All dead.'

There was one thing only that could have lured the ragged villagers down to the ruins in the days following the disaster.

Greed.

While thieves and church-robbers and hellions such as Charron and Bester had come here from time to time to risk their lives in the search for treasures, the citizens – who so often went to sleep with the sounds of the old church groaning in the night as the Magdalena chewed relentlessly away at its underpinnings – considered even their own hungry and ragged lives far too precious to risk them down there by the river.

But when the high waters finally subsided they quickly discovered one could dig and scrabble and hunt amongst the ruins almost in total safety – and so they hunted day and night.

A few were rewarded with gold and silver, although never nearly as much as they believed Santa Catarina had held to her secret bosom.

The searchers also found several corpses, and an intriguing mystery.

Everyone knew that nine men had perished,

crushed, drowned and unrecognizable.

Yet the corpses they recovered numbered but eight. . . .

CHAPTER 2

KILLER MAN

Young Ike Canby whispered, 'What is it, Dad?' Then, too excited and eager to wait for the answer, he hissed, 'Do you reckon it's him?'

'Hush, boy, just hush up, Goddamnit!'

Dad Canby, who'd been around Legend Ranch for as long as anyone could recall, stood rigid in the night, right hand wrapped tightly around the stock of his Winchester repeater. As taut as a fiddle string, the old man stared off towards the vast clump of brush that bulged out of Crockett Canyon, some two hundred yards distant. Elsewhere on the homestead acres, other men were watching and waiting for the same thing – a first glimpse of the 'Circus Bear'.

It seemed nobody from Sherman Stellarman and his guest from south of the border – the former enemy, for now at least, a friend Don Miguel Mariano of Mexico – down to the lowliest ranch hand could quite believe that the big get-together to celebrate one full year of peace between the former cattle king enemies, had just happened to coincide with the return of Star County's most renowned and unpredictable critter to the home acres, a long eighteen months since its last visit.

There were no bears native to that region of the Southwest, but the so-called Circus Bear had seemed to take on the task of rectifying that situation since busting loose from a travelling show five years earlier, and settling down to stay.

It was a big black bear, cunning as a snake and dangerous as a train wreck – or at least so said those who'd hunted and had been tormented by the critter over the years.

Dad Canby and his clan had come up from Mexico when the bear was first sighted, and the rugged old professional hunter was about the most dedicated enemy the critter had. Right now he could feel the hair rising on the back of his neck as he stood in the brush waiting to see which would appear first – the black bear or the new moon.

The latter won.

Up through the planted pines surrounding the great house rose a huge yellow moon, surely as big a moon as ever looked down on the Southwest – a hunter's moon.

The hounds strained on their leashes, and hidden men with rifles waited and watched as the spread was bathed in yellow gold, everyone bursting with impatience now including Sherman Stellarman, never normally a man to display much emotion.

Nobody was much surprised when Dad Canby, after warning everyone to hold their place and their trigger fingers, suddenly couldn't hold back any longer and squaring his jaw defiantly, sprang from cover like a teenage roustabout and bellowed deafeningly, 'Loose them lousy dogs if that's what it takes to shake this yellow-guts critter out of his hidey hole!'

Later, men argued that the bear, already regarded as about the smartest critter in Texas or Mexico, must have taken offence at the old man's disrespect, for even before the dogs could be unleashed, five hundred pounds of electrifyingly fast black bear exploded from a stand of cottonwoods downslope, just where nobody figured it to be.

The bear appeared on all fours, a black mass of blurring speed. Just beyond gun range, the critter suddenly reared up and roared. If the Circus Bear had appeared big before, now he appeared truly immense, trumpeting his defiance of Stellarman, his important guests from south of the border, every man and woman on the place and old Dan in particular.

Then, quicker than the quickest, he was down again – big, black and mean as the Devil, vanishing into the ravine and making for the river.

Within moments the hitherto empty slopes of the headquarters hill were alive with men afoot, on horseback, clutching the leads of yelping hounds – all rushing downhill like they were starving and just heard the dinner gong.

The Circus Bear led them a merry chase.

The beast had been around almost the length of a regular bear's lifetime, and had learned every trick and technique of survival in a hostile and bear-less land.

Cunning and crafty, it never killed more steers than it could eat, and it knew more tricks, hidey-holes and ways of seemingly vanishing into thin air than any other wild critter ever encountered in southwest Texas and beyond.

Up on the gallery of the great house, where Stellarmans mixed easily with Marianos, there was any amount of excitement and wagering on the outcome of what only just one or two wise heads viewed as an uneven contest – favouring the Circus Bear.

The mistress of Legend Ranch was one of this minority.

Dyana Stellarman stood alone in her lamplit window directly above the gallery, arms folded, dark eyes following the excitement. A tall and slender woman in her mid-forties, and still considered one of the great beauties of the Southwest at that time of her life, the wife of Sherman Stellarman and his four grown sons and a daughter saw it all, were amused by it all, but not necessarily involved with all that was taking place here tonight, whether it be the mad chase after the bear or the exuberant socializing directly below where she stood in her window.

She was no snob but enjoyed her own company. Of course what both pleased and relieved her was that peace had finally come between Legend and Palo Pinto, yet she still preferred to enjoy it largely from arm's length rather than be too intimately involved.

This was expected and accepted, for the cattle king's handsome wife had been very much her own woman with a steely mind of her own from the day she'd arrived here as Stellarman's bride, and the years of achievement, conflict and sometimes high drama since had not essentially changed her, even though virtually any observer of the Stellarman clan might have expected that it should, or would.

Meeting Dyana Stellarman for the first time tonight, acting out the role of wife, mother, friend and matriarch, a stranger would surely find it difficult to imagine the turmoil and high drama which had exploded into her life on the great ranch more than twenty years earlier.

She was then the seemingly proud and happy wife and mother of three healthy children, wanting for nothing, strong, accomplished and sure of her world and her position in it.

Until the day she met and fell in love with – not some railroad tycoon or Texan cattle baron – but rather a handsome Mexican outlaw who burst into her immaculate life like a Texas twister. It seemed an indecently short space of time before Antonio Villanova had seemingly almost effortlessly charmed her into turning her elegant back upon husband, children and cattle kingdom for a life beyond the law in Mexico with her dashing sixgunner, and eventually an illegitimate son of their own. . . .

'Mother?'

The voice jolted her from her reverie and she turned to see Chance walking towards her. The woman smiled, something she rarely did. Not everyone liked or understood the Stellarman matriarch, but those few who did knew her as a woman of uncommon strength and dignity, who, as history would readily attest, ran her own race and made her own pathway through life, regardless.

Dyana's other sons sometimes complained that Chance was her favorite. She denied this whenever the subject arose, yet it was true. She had a working marriage with her husband, was a loyal and loving mother to her other sons and daughter. But with Chance it had always been special. The two, mother and son, had enjoyed a rare kind of symbiosis right from the day of Chance's birth, and she would never try to explain that, or apologize for it, to anyone for any reason.

She linked her arm through his as they passed through to the crowded balcony where many of the guests were straining to follow whatever was taking place downslope, where the graceful rangeland acres came up against brush-based Bald Knob, rising incongruously against the new moon.

'What do you think, mother?' Chance smiled. 'Will they or won't they?'

'You know my opinion on that, honey.'

'Which is – you think that bear is smarter than anyone who tries to nail it?'

'Exactly.'

'That's not showing much confidence in your own kinfolk, guests or Dad Canby.'

'They've all chased that fine animal before, and every single time he's survived to torment them another day. Believe me, the Circus Bear knows there is a big function taking place here tonight and he deliberately held back his appearance in order to make Legend look foolish in the eyes of the whole county when they fail to bag him.'

Chance laughed, turning to go.

'You're a cynical, cruel woman, and just to put you in your place I'm going to join the hunt and make sure we've got that black pelt pegged out on the hayshed wall come midnight.'

'Ten dollars says it won't be.'

'That's a bet,' he called back, and was gone, her eyes not leaving him until his tall frame dropped from sight. Then she joined her daughter and settled down to watch the contest she still believed had been organized by a dumb beast and not that noisy yelling mob down there chasing it through the brush.

The hunters were concentrating on the brushline over by the dam, when action exploded in the exact opposite direction two hundred yards distant.

The bear had gained full speed charging down-slope behind the cover of the trees, now, with seeming defiance, exploded briefly into sight and streaked across some fifty yards of open rangeland only to vanish again in the timber before one hunter could get a bead on it.

'Loose the goddamn hounds!' old Dad hollered, and now the time had come for the dogs to run they ran like fury, rushing down into the timberline of the gulch with men of all shapes and sizes, many in dinner suits, pouring after them holding glinting weapons high.

The bear led them a breathless chase, and by the time Chance and his brother Travis arrived on the scene from the house, it had disappeared yet again.

Dad paused to fire his rifle off in sheer frustration and the derisive cheers and jeers coming from the well-refreshed spectators from higher up did nothing to soothe his frustration.

It took some nerve to rib Dad Canby, even if this was a festive occasion filled with boisterous cheer and goodwill. As graceless and primitive as a mud turtle, Dad nonetheless held great respect as a tracker, trailsman and occasionally manhunter.

It was in this latter capacity this hardy man had gained wide fame and admiration when he led a huge posse on the trail of one of the most dangerous desperadoes ever to come out of Texas.

Unfortunately for Texas and Sonora, the posse's capture of the killer had been followed almost immediately by Charron's escape, leaving dead men in his wake. Charron had since gone on to play his bloody role in the region, had at times even hired his gun to the Marianos when their feud with Legend Ranch erupted into flame.

But had Charron the killer shown up suddenly there tonight, Dad Canby would not have given him a second look. He was obsessed with this bear and had boasted that this would be the day he finally nailed him.

'I want two good riders to get in there and cut him off from the river!' he bawled, whirling about and almost falling. 'Where in tarnation are Travis and Chance?'

The answer to that was – gone.

At that moment the brothers were deep in the pines to the left, racing along an old animal path which led down to the lower dam. It was Travis' hunch, based on past experience with the bear, that he would dive in there, swim across and then lose himself on Bald Knob where he could not be pursued.

His hunch proved to be right, and by the time they were in sight of the dam, with several other hunters galloping from the timber off to their right, the Circus Bear was visible below, ploughing through the water at tremendous speed.

Travis touched off a shot but Chance kept riding fast and was a hundred yards ahead of the nearest huntsman as the bear emerged on the far side. He reined in, threw his rifle to his shoulder and pulled the trigger.

Everyone saw the white plume of dam water rise – a good fifty feet behind the fast-moving bear.

'What's wrong with you?' roared Travis, red-faced and hectic as he sawed to a halt at his side. 'That's the worst shot you ever fired, and you've fired plenty—'

The man's words were swallowed by another crash

of the rifle. This time, the bullet smacked rocky ground just yards behind the dripping mass of shining black fury that was the Circus Bear.

'Unbelievable!' Travis yelled, finally getting his long rifle to his shoulder – the same second their quarry was swallowed by the giant boulders that littered the base of Bald Knob.

Gone!

Upslope some one hundred yards, Dad Canby seemed in danger of a fatal seizure. 'My Aunt Grace could've swatted that critter with a wash towel from that distance!' he choked. 'Or run it down in her wheelchair!'

'You . . . you missed on purpose!' Travis Stellarman was even taller than Chance, ten years older and was not renowned for holding back when angered. He pushed his blowing horse closer to his brother. 'All right, you've got a reason, I know. You've always got some kind of dumbass reason for everything you do. But you tell me . . . why didn't you nail that critter that's been eating Legend beeves for ten years. C'mon, you're the talker . . . I'm waiting, mister!'

'I guess I just figured there had been enough killing, Tray.'

'Huh?'

Chance gestured as a bunch of riders including Don Mariano's son, Virgil, clattered up to rein in.

'Look around and tell me I'm wrong,' he said, loud enough for all to hear. 'After years of feuding between Legend and Palo Pinto Rancho we finally

28

get to make peace once and for all, and for the first time ever the Marianos family has come to Legend as friends. That's a mighty big occasion, brother, and what makes it even bigger by far, is the news that Charron is dead. So, all in all, I guess I elected to spread the peace a little wider to cover the bear.'

Travis Stellarman's jaw dropped. In the background, Dad Canby looked up at the moon and appeared about to weep. Heads turned as hoofbeats sounded and they saw two riders coming down from the tree line, both riding side-saddle.

Young Virgil Mariano gaped. He'd never seen the girl he hoped to marry on horseback, hadn't known she could even ride. Yet nobody was surprised to see Mrs Stellarman atop her tall and spirited hack, which she brought in neatly to rein up alongside her sons.

'Now, ma, don't you horn in on this—' Travis began, but the woman spoke over him in a voice that carried authority.

'Supper is waiting, gentlemen. You will all kindly join Mr Stellarman and myself in the dining-room . . . immediately.'

When Mrs Stellarman used that tone, people heeded. Travis plainly wasn't happy as he swung his mount about and used spur, but he uttered not a word. And once the strong man of the Legend was heading obediently upslope, there was certainly nobody else prepared to dispute the iron lady of Legend Ranch.

It proved a brilliant night from there on in, a night of excitement, goodwill, friendship and music which continued on until mid-morning before the last tottering reveller vanished to his quarters, leaving only the cleaning staff and Chance Stellarman still abroad.

Taking a last cigarette on the gallery before turning in himself, Chance had much to occupy his thoughts, particularly the fact that this long-awaited night of peace and reconciliation between old rangeland enemies had coincided almost to the day with the news of the violent death in Mexico of Legend's deadliest enemy and the most dangerous man the border lands had ever known.

And Charron was his name.

CHAPTER 3

MATADOR

It was a small, barefoot boy who first sighted the horseman riding down out of the pass into Los Santos through the drowsing morning sunlight.

Immediately the urchin put on a big welcoming smile and moved out into the crown of the road in the hope of a few centavos. There was a bullfight scheduled to be staged in the town's ramshackle bull-ring that afternoon, and visitors could often prove soft touches for the town's junior beggars.

'Welcome, *señor*.'

The urchin made himself appear cute and appealing as only a hungry, street-wise gutter kid knew how. Yet his pleading voice suddenly faded as he got a clear look at that face above him with cigar clamped between white teeth, brilliant black eyes cut to a single steely gleam beneath the shadow of a sombrero that had seen better days.

Swiftly, knowingly, the boy's wide eyes took in the matching sixshooters in their holsters and the notches carved into the white-handled butts.

Dios mio! How many notches were there?

The kid was off in a twinkling of thin brown legs, chilled as he rarely was by the summer wind that might blow into the dusty streets of Los Santos.

Gaining the security of the high dry weeds lining the road, the boy considered the hard truth that there were still many things in the world of adults that could puzzle and even scare him. He knew he had such a long way to go before he would ever be man enough to be able to stare such a *hombre* in the eye.

The horseman rode a short distance then halted to look over the town. Charron had never visited this place set deep in the hook of the Rio Magdalena before, and that was the main reason he had elected to come here today rather than other places in the region which boasted their own rings, but where he might be known.

The last time Charron's name had hit the headlines was the report of his death in the cave-in of the Church of Santa Catarina in a humble border village in the next province.

Los Santos mainly comprised a long, rough street fronted by adobe buildings and intersected six times by dusty cross streets. The place boasted one huge general store, several cantinas, a law office that had been closed down for over a year and a church that had been shut down even longer.

And, of course, there was the bullring.

The horseman's black eyes studied the ramshackle structure on the far edge of town, and a sneer curled his lip. Before the lure of the sixguns had drawn him away to the wider world of man killing, he would never have deigned to display his other major talent, fighting the bulls, in such a town as this even for a sack of gold.

For two years of his teenage life, he had fought and often starred in the finest bullrings in the land.

Things were different now. These times the name 'Charron' was far more likely to be heard mentioned in low dives or in outlaw hideouts and in the law offices across the country, rather than in the bull-rings of Mexico.

The one still often known as 'The Matador' would fight bulls only whenever it appealed to him these days, frequently risking all for a pittance, at times for nothing at all. He needed the bullfighting from time to time, for he had to prove to himself that he could still do it. Kill. Be brave. Conquer your own fear. Still be a man.

But there was added reason for his appearance here this drowsy Los Santos day.

He glanced down at his right leg. It was stiff in the extended stirrup, and his boot jutted out from the horse's flank. The leg injury was just one of many suffered in that nightmare cave-in of the Church of Santa Catarina.

All his henchmen had perished within the first hour of the collapse. His life had been saved initially by a twenty-foot pillar which fell at an angle above him, leaving him room to breathe and move about. It was all the advantage a man of his iron will needed. He immediately set out, with floodwater lapping up to his jaw, to tunnel his way out through mud, stone and plaster where one false move could mean instant death, and where there was only darkness and a silence as deep as the grave.

Time had no meaning. He was only to learn after breaking through to fresh air and sunlight that he'd been entombed for six days and nights.

He emerged more dead than alive yet still found both the will and strength to drag his ravaged body fifteen miles to the next village before seeking help. For he was a church-robber and bandit gun-killer who might well get himself lynched were he to be found near the place where he had helped destroy Agua Prieta's ancient church.

Recovery had been slow. But at least the medico in Morado was sober and reasonably proficient, and he soon found a lonely widow who took him in and fed him chicken soup and slipped into his bed at night.

Even so, it was still the better part of a month before he was able to climb on to a horse. He rode round the village for a further ten days to build up his strength before cleaning out the widow's life savings and heading north-west.

He chose that direction on account he was unknown in that region and needed someplace anonymous where he might get to fully rest up and recover from his injuries before making any decisions on what his next moves would and should be.

And riding slowly north he was willing his body back to health with the iron will that stemmed from the survival of a brutal childhood where one fought for every mouthful simply for the 'privilege' of keeping alive.

That life force surged within him when, some days later, he watched the play of light over the faded canvas covers and sad old buildings of the bullring of Morado.

Half closing his eyes, he drifted back in time to the village of his early days that had been the closest thing the killer ever came to experiencing a childhood.

It was there he had grown from homeless orphan to early youth upon the diseased and plague-ridden streets. And there, also, that he was to eventually master the craft of the matador, going out at night with his friends to the great bull-breeding ranchos to face the giant beasts which had been bred to hate all mankind and to kill whenever they might.

Few of Charron's contemporaries had persevered long with these illicit 'bullfights'; several had died or been crippled in pursuit of the dream to become a hero-matador. Yet one boy who had been equally as reckless, brave and persistent as himself was now the principal matador in the bullrings of Mexico City. Charron had believed then, as he did now, that he was the superior fighter of the two, was sure he might have proven this in time had he not been diverted by the lure of the gun.

In bullfighting you killed only animals. He discovered an even greater talent for killing men.

Yet he had persisted against the bulls – watching the real matadors whenever he got the chance, then mimicking their grace, skill and courage in his illicit nightly bouts out at the ranchos. Where his awed young companions would softly call: 'Charron! Charron!' as he caped and confused a snorting man-killer beneath the Mexican moonlight, over time establishing a name which one day would be heard in the great rings, a fame he was never fully to achieve until he buckled on the guns.

He finished off his cigar and flipped the stub away before nudging his mount back towards the village center.

There was a festive air about Los Santos, and large families of peons had been drifting in since first light. None paid any particular attention to the slender black-haired rider who tied up his horse to a saloon close by the ring, and walked with a slowly improving limp through the eager crowds, headed for the cantina. Just another handsome drifter come to town to watch the fights, they thought, obviously poor, likely harmless.

It was noisy in the cantina. The smoke-filled air was thick with voices, the deep-throated strumming of guitars and the excited speculation upon the outcome of the afternoon's drama to come.

Charron recognized a few familiar faces from his more active 'Matador' days. But he averted his face and no one recognized him.

The big low-roofed room was pleasantly cool and dim, smelling of tobacco smoke, rotgut booze and unwashed humanity. He loved it. They were the scents, sounds and sights of his earlier life.

Behind the main bar hung a grimed and smoke-yellowed oil painting of two buxom young women embracing upon a silk couch.

Charron turned his back on the picture and thought of her. High-born Alma Mariano, daughter of Don Mariano who had once hired his gun in the long war of attrition against Legend Ranch, had spurned his attentions in favor of Chance Stellarman, the man he hated most as a result. Rejection had left a bitter taste in the mouth of a man who by nature hated to lose.

But of course all such problems were solvable for a gun king. He would see Stellarman dead and Alma in his bed in the fullness of time. Of this he was certain.

'But one thing at a time, "Matador",' he warned himself. First he would challenge the brave bulls here, which would tell him as only they could if he was still the brave *hombre* he had been before he'd been crushed and all but buried alive. . . .

The tiered seats of the plaza de toros were beginning to fill as the handsome stranger with the limp presented himself along with a handful of other hopefuls to the bullring's promoter in his musty little office beneath the main stand.

The early fights today would be mainly for the *novilleros*, and the bulls selected would be inferior animals. This made these often bloody contests somewhat more equal, yet Charron knew there could be just as much high risk for a tyro in such contests as there was for a prima matador in the great stadia of Mexico City.

The seedy promoter thought Charron appeared likely enough until he noticed the limp, and shook his head.

'I have merely strained a muscle, *señor*,' Charron pleaded, holding his hat to his chest. 'As I warm to the fight the stiffness shall be gone, I promise you.'

The man just shook his head but stopped when Charron plucked down an ornamental sword from a wall bracket. Watched by the promoter and several hopefuls, he next proceeded to slash to pieces a gaudy wall poster of a bullfight, displaying quite the most elegant exhibition of lightning sword play the man had ever seen.

'I think perhaps I should worry more about my poor bulls than you,' the man joked as Charron signed a fake name to his contract.

He would receive a paltry twenty pesos for each bull he fought.

He half-smiled as he quit the dingy office. How the mighty had fallen!

One hour later, Charron stood quietly behind the stout wooden barricade flanking the ring as the corrida got under way.

'*Ole, Antonio! Ole!*'

The crowd was soon giving encouragement to the local boy. He needed it all, Charron thought with a sneer. Flatfooted and awkward, yet showing some genuine foolish courage and the brutish style of an abbattoir slaughterman – that was home-grown Antonio.

Yet the novice finally killed his bull and the loyal home crowd cheered lustily. Then it was the turn of the stranger who had given the name, Chico.

The promoter, moving up to the main bunting-draped box to join the owner, a visiting matador from the south and several local dignitaries, immediately noted that Chico had not shaken off the limp, as promised. He started sweating. If this went badly, the crowd might riot and guess who would be blamed? And when the chute gate was opened and the red bull came storming out into the ring, he was obliged to reach for his bottle of absinthe to steady the nerves.

Charron advanced casually out into the center, sizing up the bull with an expert eye. Bigger and meaner-looking than anticipated, but likely stupid. He hoped he was right about that.

Man and beast exchanged stares. The crowd hushed. The red cape fluttered and the bull lowered its head and charged.

Charron stood with feet close together and drew the cape across his body with confidence and grace. The bull thundered by him very close. Charron lifted the cape at the last moment to make the beast rear, tiring itself.

The crowd fell silent.

This novice seemed to know what he was doing.

Charron completed several perfect passes before his leg began to fail. Sweat was coursing down his face as he made his way back to the barricades to collect his sword. The crowd cheered enthusiastically, recognizing skill and courage when they saw it.

'*Olé*!' a fat man bellowed, standing up. '*Viva* El Rengo!'

El Rengo. The lame!

Charron froze. Even though he was noticeably limping by this, and the yelling of the mob was affectionate, he still felt the anger rise. He couldn't help it. He would kill a man for mocking him, had done so in the past.

A red mist clouded his vision as he moved back to center ring. He tried to suppress his rage but only partly succeeded. Then the bull was coming at him with the speed of an express train. 'Concentrate on the animal, Charron! Let the mob anger you and you could die here!'

He very nearly did.

'Son of a whore!' he taunted the onrushing beast and was making the imperfect pass with the muleta when the horn hooked into his short braided jacket.

He was unhurt but was hurled to the ground!

Other *novilleros* came rushing to his aid as he struggled erect, flapping their capes to drag the beast away. White with rage, Charron ordered them away, then cursed as the bull got by them and he only succeeded in dodging its angry rush by inches.

Even though his anger was threatening to consume him completely, he had enough clear-headedness left to realize there was no chance of his winning this bout now – that the matador who faced any bull with his temper out of control was halfway to begging for death.

The others again distracted the beast with their capes, enabling the limping, ashen-faced novice to limp off to the security of the barricades. Despite the distracting capes, the bull came after him yet again, seeming to shake the arena with the impact of his horns against the stout timbers. Then, above the racket, he heard the ugliest sound on earth to a man with too great a vanity and pride – the sound of laughter.

'El Rengo! El Rengo!' they chanted as the bull continued to assault the barrier. 'Come out, El Rengo, the first matador!' Mocking him. Humiliation!

He was half-blind as he limped across to his belongings just inside the doorway. He fumbled a moment then reappeared with a Colt Peacemaker in either fist, one of which was used to swipe an attendant aside when the man made to detain him.

Next moment the crowd was hushing as he appeared in full view, lunging and limping towards the bull which now stood alone in center ring, twitching its tail and emitting short gusty snorts of anger.

In that sucked-out moment of silence which suddenly encompassed the ring, the crowd realized the man's intention as he closed the gap to the bull, which lowered its head to charge.

41

Guns against a brave fighting bull? Infamous thought!

The bull charged and Charron's revolvers filled the arena with explosions of angry sound.

The skull of a bull is as hard as concrete. Charron knew this. He directed his bullets elsewhere, to the chest, the legs, the face, his cutters chattering now with the rapidity of a Gatling gun at ever decreasing range.

His bullets tore the animal apart. It was already dying, bloody and brave, as it crashed to the crimsoned sand. The man was not satisfied. Lunging across to the creature he rammed a muzzle down its throat and jerked trigger twice more.

So great was the shock to the onlookers that the limping matador had almost reached the exit beneath the stands, smoking cutters already swiftly reloaded, before they recovered.

An attendant attempted to block his path to the stables and he blew a black hole in the man's forehead, kicking him in the face as he fell.

He was clambering astride his horse before the belated vast roar of rage shook the stadium end to end. His expression did not change as raking spurs saw his mount shoot into the open space beyond the stands, where angry men were rushing to halt him.

The bucking guns in his hands stormed and killed and stormed again.

In an instant, the sound of the mob switched from righteous rage to total terror. Suddenly everyone was

42

diving to ground, screaming that a madman was on the loose.

True enough.

But this madman knew exactly what he was doing. Rage, slaughter and flight were nothing new to 'The Matador'. Raking savagely with steel, he blasted everything in his path, and the wild-eyed horse was travelling at a flat gallop by the time he went roaring through the exit gate.

Not a hand was laid on the killer before he was gone. Much later, they would compare the group photographs of the *novilleros* taken by the management's cameraman prior to the festivities, and the shocked *teniente* would compare them against his rogue's gallery of wanted outlaws and realize they had been visited by one of the hellions 'killed' in that murderous business at Agua Prieta several weeks earlier. The one named Charron.

By that time the killer was in the high country and once again fully restored to his customary cold, clear calm. For he had learned, that bloody afternoon, that even though he might never again fight the bulls with his old, easy skills, he could still kill men. Better than ever.

Ole, Charron!

On Legend Ranch, some arguments blew up fast and could blow away even faster. Some dragged on for days. This one looked like being a stayer.

'Any man who doesn't believe that Charron coming back from the dead – again – doesn't mean

43

trouble is about to break out all over,' Travis Stellarman opined, 'is just a goddamned ostrich.'

'Any man who reckons it does mean trouble,' younger brother Lafe countered, 'is a man who wants the war to start up again.'

The brothers traded glares where they stood by the horse corrals in the late afternoon. Dad Canby and his boys had run in a colt for breaking, and the Legend's regular team of Monroe and Shorthorn were already busy at what they did best, horse-breaking.

Or at least diminutive Shorthorn was – he'd just been thrown by the spirited colt for the third time. Portly Monroe, the self styled brains of the partnership, occasionally offered some expert advice from the safety of the top rail.

'You know something, kid?' Travis said after a weighty pause.

'What?' Lafe was not as cocky as he sounded. He rarely had the grit to stand up to his big brother. Not only did Travis outweigh him by forty pounds, he had been born bossy and seemed to grow more so every year.

Travis reached out and poked him in the sternum. 'You are beginning to act and sound more like Chance every day, is what.'

'I take that as a compliment.'

'Oh, I'm goddamn sure you do.' Travis' tone was caustic. 'I mean, they don't call you two the 'Hand In Glove Kids' for nothing, do they?'

The youngest male Stellarman flushed hotly. That nickname belonged to the past. Travis and Carter had hatched it up at the time when Chance and Lafe first spoke up against the ongoing conflict between Legend and Palo Pinto. That was a long time ago now. Carter was dead, and it was a long time since the Palo Pinto's former top gunfighter had last fought against the Legend. The Stellarman spread had recently celebrated the report of Charron's 'death' in a church collapse in Mexico, only to have the shadow of the killer fall across the Southwest again after the pistolero had been allegedly identified as alive and as lethal as ever following a chaotic blood-bath in a bullring south of the border.

But Lafe Stellarman regarded himself as a boy no longer, he was insisting they stop treating him like one.

'One of these days, Travis—' he warned hotly, but the other cut him off.

'Ahh, forget it, kid, I didn't really mean it.' The big man tugged at his thick mustache. 'But it's just that deep down I know that with that butchering bastard coming back from the grave the way they claim he has, I wouldn't wager hard money that Don Miguel mightn't hire him to give us some hell again. I mean, peace treaties or not, Miguel and the old man are still like a couple of old mossy-horn bulls under-neath. Matter of fact, I reckon if it wasn't for mother's influence they would never have got to the peace table anyway.'

This was quite possibly true. The cross-border feud between the two giant cattle spreads of that Rio Grande region stretched back many years. There were as many reasons put forward to support why these troubles had seemed inevitable as there had been attempts to achieve peace in that long and turbulent time.

Yet finally the peacemakers had triumphed and it was almost a year now since hostilities had ceased. Some cynics attributed this to the fact that Mariano and Stellarman had grown old and no longer had the stomach for feuding and fussing as they had as younger men. Others believed it had more to do with hired guns such as Charron either dying, getting crippled or just deciding they were too fond of living to take part in such a risky business any longer.

This latter attitude still strongly prevailed. Yet there could be no doubting that the news of Charron's 'demise' followed by the jolting report of his resurrection had stirred some old war dogs who would have been better off left sleeping.

'Damnit, Travis,' Lafe complained, 'the troubles are over. Just look at the facts. We've had the Marianos visit with us for a week like good old country neighbours, and now Chance and Alma are about to set their wedding date. Charron coming back from the grave is not going to change any of that and I reckon it's dumb to say it might just because we hear some rumor he ain't dead like we all heard he was.'

Travis suddenly jumped back from the fence as a thousand pounds of dynamite-on-the-hoof with Shoehorn perched atop him went storming by in a series of brain-jolting bucks.

'Don't be too hard on that critter's mouth there, Shoehorn!' Monroe advised from his spot high on the fence well out of harm's way.

Shoehorn's response was vivid and offensive and the two became locked in yet another of their fierce wrangles. Lafe was forced to laughter despite himself, but stopped when he saw Monroe studying him soberly.

'How old are you now, kid?' he asked. 'Seventeen? an' spoil a hoss for life iffen you harden his mouth up while he's a yearling.'

'Get typhoid, you fat shoat!' bawled the imperilled horseman. 'Turn blue!'

Accustomed to such insults, Monroe just shook his head with benign tolerance. But the horse chose to take offence instead, and plunged wickedly, twisting and kicking like a sinner in torment, eyes red and raging now.

Shoehorn immediately demonstrated why he held such a high reputation as a horse-breaker. He tightened his grip on the ribbons and actually leaned back casually in the saddle like an oldster taking his leisure in a rocking chair on the back porch. The Canby boys hollered and waved their hats in admiration, but their old dad just scowled and said nothing at all. Dad Canby had been sulking ever since he'd led the chase after that fool bear, and it could be a long time yet before he would give up on that and find something else to gripe about.

Travis coughed from the hoof-raised dust as he started away from the breaking corral with Lafe trailing him. The Stellarmans' eldest son was still brooding about their discussion.

'The trouble with you, Lafe, is you don't understand the real story behind the feud and you likely never will now things are patched up.'

'Why, I figure I know just as much as anybody else on this spread.'

Travis halted in the middle of the yard, hands on hips. His blue eyes, a Stellarman trademark, drilled at the youngest brother.

'So, what do you figure was the cause, if you know so much, kid?'

Lafe spread his hands.

'Simple. Pride, of course. Both Don Miguel and the old man wanted to be the biggest cattleman either side of the Rio. For years they have been like a couple of kids who—'

'Wrong!'

'Huh?'

'Just goes to show how little you learn from all those books you read, kid. There was just one reason behind all those years of fighting, and that was our mom.'

'How the hell do you figure that one out? You don't mean it was on account both of them was chasing after Dyana before she settled on Father?'

'Feuds have been touched off by far less than that, boy.'

The youngest Stellarman was intrigued by the notion of two impressive men in their late fifties still brawling and feuding over his mother.

But this reach back into family history reminded the youngest male Stellarman of the breadth of a great scandal from the past involving their glamorous mother, who, as did his three surviving brothers, he held almost in awe.

'Trav,' he said coaxingly, 'you said once you'd tell me the full story about Mother.'

'Tell you what, go see Chance and tell him I said it's time you were told.'

Lafe's eyes widened with excitement. 'Can't you tell the story—'

'Nope. Chance is better at this sort of thing. In any case, he's likely the only one of us who knows the whole story from start to finish.'

'How come?'

The older man made a dismissive gesture. 'You're not blind, kid. You know Mother and Chance have been close as two clams all his life. All Carter and me knew when she finally came back from Mexico, way back when, was what you already know now. Could be only Chance can give you the whole story and give it to you straight. If not him then I guess you're out of luck. You can be dead sure you'll never get it from the old man.'

'But—'

'See Chance!' Travis snapped and strode away, a big, broad-shouldered man of action who mostly left all the talking and speculating to others.

Travis found Chance in the tack room patching a bridle. Despite Travis' recommendation, he half expected his favorite brother to turn him down flat.

Instead, Chance just stood studying him in silence for a half-minute, then turned and set the saddle aside.

'OK, Lafe, just what is it you want to know about Mother and Antonio Villanova?'

The youth's eyes were wide. 'Why, everything, of course.'

'Well, let's get over to the bunkhouse. We were all sworn never to mention that chunk of family drama, but seeing as—'

'You know I've got a right to know and you're going to tell me,' Lafe cut in with sudden confidence.

'Guess I am at that. Okay, follow me, noseybones.'

CHAPTER 4

OUT OF THE PAST

The story began on a quiet spring morning in south-western Texas when the horseman showed coming in across the top forty. . . .

Nobody on Legend Ranch had ever sighted Antonio Villanova before and only one or two had ever heard the man from Mexico's name mentioned. Elric Mogg the line-rider had heard something of a man with a similar name being involved in a shootout, while Roscoe Hinch the ranch smithy claimed a Mexican provendor to the Legend had once made reference to a 'Villanova' having been involved in a bank holdup in Three Deuces.

But these details only surfaced after it was all too late.

Villanova, most likely the most dashing and personable Mexican the spread had ever seen, with his flashing eyes and winning personality, was pack-

51

ing lead in his shoulder as a result of an 'accident' while loading his sixgun.

Western hospitality demanded he be taken in and cared for until he recovered, which roughly took three weeks.

That proved more than long enough for the stately Stellarman wife and mother of two to fall head-over-heels in love with the man who seemed to represent everything her older and conservative husband was not.

Sherman Stellarman was a former Civil War colonel who still looked and acted the part years later. Tall, autocratic and humourless, he was nonetheless a man of strength and character who, unwisely as it eventuated, seemed to believe that merely permitting Dyana Halliday to have become his wife and mother of his children was enough to ensure her life-long gratitude and devotion.

The cattle king failed to recognize the signs and signals indicating his stunning young wife was finding her role as wife and mother beyond reproach, increasingly stifling and demeaning.

Nor did he even notice the increasing amount of time Dyana seemed to spend with the recovering Mexican during those weeks. On a personal level, the cattle king regarded Villanova as far too flashy, cocksure and much too popular with everybody on the spread for a charity case, and would be pleased to see the back of him as soon as he was capable of riding out.

As Chance related it to Lafe, having heard the

story from his mother's own lips, Dyana Stellarman had fallen for the swashbuckling Mexican almost from the first. He'd brought a breath of something wild and unknown, was a romantic figure of mystery with a flashing smile and boundless youth so much in contrast with the somber and humourless husband who at most times seemed to act like a stern father more than a loving spouse.

By the end of that first week Dyana knew that when Villanova left she would be with him.

She would miss her children desperately; what loving mother would not? But always a woman of fierce passions and an almost masculine contempt for danger or risk, she was able to reassure herself that Travis and Carter would be reared correctly and carefully without her, and hopefully one day would follow their own destinies wherever they might lead them, just as she was now following hers.

The couple left for Mexico in the dead of the night and within weeks were living together in Jicarilla Province. Dyana was pregnant with their son, Richard Rodrigo, born months later while she was high in the sierras running from the *Rurales* with Villanova and his gang – and loving every dangerous moment.

By this, Lafe was agog. All he'd ever heard of the scandal were fragments and snippets. Chance's recounting sounded like the complete vivid story starkly told.

Chance lit up and continued:

The little family survived the sierras and many a

53

subsequent perilous adventure, including one where her husband led fifteen men south to strike a major blow at Palo Pinto, then pushed on south to conduct a wide search for his runaway wife.

They were never found and may have remained lost and anonymous for all time but for a seemingly innocent incident which resulted in death and cruel loss.

The disaster began in Baroyeca innocently enough.

Villanova the desperado was riding into the Sota Hills for a genial reunion with an old fellow renegado, Rael Zamparello, and some of their henchmen from the old days. At the last moment little Richard cried and wanted to accompany him. The loving father agreed, and in doing so signed both their death warrants.

The outlaws met as arranged. What neither knew was that a squadron of *Rurales* had been tagging Zamparello's party for several days. In the resulting ambush, Dyana's husband and son were shot to death along with Zamparello and his five-strong band of desperadoes, their corpses subsequently drenched in oil and burned to cinders as a warning to all outlaws.

It never entered Dyana's mind to return to Texas. She had made her choices freely and willingly and would live by them. In a place like Baroyeca, there was only one way an impoverished but attractive American woman could make her living, and Dyana was still the star attraction at the Baroyeca bordello when her husband rescued her and took her back to Legend Ranch two years later.

'Since then mother and father have been as solid together as they were before Villanova rode in across that paddock yonder, Lafe,' Chance concluded, twisting a cigarette into shape with deft fingers. He half smiled. 'Nothing had changed. The old man always thought he was boss here, but the rest of us knew mother was smarter, stronger and gutsier than he ever knew how to be. And that's how it's been from that day to this.'

He lit up, drew deep, studied his brother.

'So, can you take all that or not, kid?'

'Phew . . . I don't know what to say, man. . . .'

Chance rose and laughed easily.

'Could be best to just leave it that way, bro. Like how I did when Travis finally told me. It's all in the past and best left that way. Agreed?'

The boy's head was still ringing. What he had just heard was shocking, he supposed, yet somehow exhilarating. His serene and seemingly invincible mother and a crazy Mex gunslinger? Who'd have ever thought it?

Suddenly life on Legend didn't appear nearly as boring as it had seemed ever since the range war ended.

The brothers quit the building and headed back for the breaking yards with Lafe feeling excited to be a Stellarman again and wished fervently things might continue that way. It was a fervent wish from the heart – yet one that would come back to mock him before he and his family and their kingdom of grass and cattle were many days older.

Legend Ranch lay beneath a blanket of moonlight and the ranch house blazed with lamplight.

Beyond the bunkhouses, corrals and stable the spidery windmill clanked away in the night, twisting ceaselessly to meet the face of the wind, a familiar and comforting sound to sleeping cattle and drowsy men alike.

Chance Stellarman saw a whiteface calf lift its head to the newly risen moon, a splash of white against the dark mass of the herd out on the south pasture.

This was everything Legend meant to him now – peace, tranquillity and the reassurance of old, long-established customs, rituals and truths. In his boyhood years he had never understood why the old Stellarman hands and Sleeper Logan had almost seemed to prefer battle, hatred and the eternal stench of gunsmoke to this sort of peace.

Yet now he himself was a man with his own dead men behind him and scars upon his young body. He knew life could never be as simple as you saw it when young. Wanting peace – but wanting it with honor were two very different things. Those old gun hands from the early days had understood that peace and tranquillity came at a price.

'Chance?'

He turned at the sound of his sister's voice. Melanie had come out to join him and his mother at this favored old meeting place. The girl insisted mother and brother come inside for supper, but neither showed any interest.

Melanie pouted. She was still just a kid, he thought affectionately, even if she was every day beginning to look more and more a young woman.

'But, Chance, I'm hungry.'

'But we're not, Mel . . . simple as that.'

'Why don't you ever take me seriously, Chance Stellarman?'

He had to laugh. Everything was so serious for the youngest Stellarman these days. As Melanie had blossomed this year, suddenly young men from surrounding spreads around the region began stopping by on all sorts of pretexts to visit. But she was still a child, he told himself soberly, and understood why she should be disturbed secretly by all this concern about the killer Charron and his 'resurrection from the dead.'

Studying his only sister, Chance wondered if he had ever been that young and carefree.

His face darkened.

In his mind's eye there appeared the image of a two-gun killer as handsome as he was deadly. Many years earlier down along the Rio Grande with Sleeper Logan, he had first heard Charron described as the son of the devil. Chance was not superstitious or easily scared. In those times he'd refused to see Charron as anything but a man just like everyone else, even when some of his more infamous deeds caused others to question that view.

That was before Charron had come to face down

Sleeper Logan.

And well before the black day Charron slaughtered his brother Carter and went on to take the lives
of the dozen Legend riders he'd burned to death in
a brush blaze in a dead-end canyon in the Rio
Isabella region of Chihuahua.

So many men, good, bad and normal had
perished at his hand over the years. . . .

More than once Chance had counted the killer
dead. Yet even recently when an entire church
collapsed upon the killer's head and took all his
henchmen to their final judgment, the two-gun
slaughter man had reappeared to kill and kill again.

Was it any wonder that this latest news weighed
heavily upon his shoulders on such a tranquil night?
Sure, he still believed Charron to be just a man. But
might he possibly yet prove to be the man capable of
destroying this life which embraced him so peace-
fully and vividly tonight?

Dyana finally spoke from the shadows.

'You go on ahead and tell cook we'll be in soon,
Melanie. Chance and I still have a couple of things to
discuss here, honey.'

'Heavens, mother, you've been out here for
absolutely hours! How could you possibly have
anything left to talk about?'

Their only response was tolerant smiles. 'Very
well,' she sighed, moving off. 'I'll tell cook ten
minutes. But then I expect you to spend some time
with me, Chance Stellarman. If you don't teach me to
do that new dance step before the Cattleman's Ball

on Friday I'll be too embarrassed to attend!'

Chance smiled as her slender figure receded across the dew-damp grass. But the expression faded quickly. This was a serious night for all its beauty.

Mother and son rose together and Dyana linked her arm through his. They started slowly towards the lights, mother and son still held close by a bond that had existed all their lives despite their markedly different personalities. While Chance displayed a genial and easy-going persona which concealed a steely strength, Dyana was the unchallenged queen and matriarch of Legend who had sewn her youthful wild oats as flamboyantly as any woman ever had, yet had survived it to eventually return to her former position as the real power behind the throne in this kingdom of grass and cattle.

They were very alike underneath, Chance knew, sharing common strongly-held attitudes which often set them at loggerheads with Sherman and Travis.

Dyana and Chance had always argued for peace on Legend and an end to the long war of attrition with Palo Pinto. Sherman and his elder sons had always accepted the long-running range war as a fact of border life, not all that different from the weather or the fluctuating stock market.

Nonetheless, he must concede, both men had made their peace with their old foe and seemed accepting if not quite completely trusting of one another now.

It had taken the recent news of a bullfighter going berserk with a sixgun in a backwater village named

Los Santos to cast a fresh cloud of uncertainty across the Stellarmans' kingdom of grasses, men and cattle.

Chance frowned thoughtfully.

The question that teased the edges of his mind was whether he believed Charron's resurrection would tempt Don Mariano to regress to his old ways. Was it remotely possible the Mexican grandee might be tempted to seek that butcher's services again? Or would he remain true to the principles of the peace treaty struck between Palo Pinto and Legend almost a year and a half ago now?

Chance felt his mother's touch on his arm. 'I would not allow you to do it, Chance.'

He glanced down at her. 'What do you mean, mother?'

'Go to Mexico, of course.'

'I didn't say anything about Mexico.'

'You didn't have to. I know you too well, my son. Ever since we heard about Charron I've seen what you are thinking in your eyes.'

'I sure don't know what you're talking about.'

She just shook her head. She thought she knew him too well at times. She might concede she was wrong about his intentions, but he could not deny he had been preoccupied with that evil news as she contended. Dead one day – killing bulls and inno-cent people the next? How could a man overlook that sort of thing?

He was pensive as they moved on.

Legend Ranch had cost Charron dear the last time he had buckled on his sixguns and ridden north out of Mexico on a mission to murder Sherman, he mused.

That reckless attempt had resulted in the Matador taking several serious gunshot wounds which had apparently seen him forced to lie up back across the Rio for several months before grabbing the headlines again with his reckless attempt at plundering that old church on Rio Magdalena.

In addition to these setbacks the killer had also lost any faint chance he may have thought he had with Alma Mariano when she become betrothed to Chance in recent months. It was a known fact that the killer had long carried a ridiculously impossible torch for the Don's daughter.

He nodded. Whichever way you looked, you came up against reason after reason why the killer's bloody appearance in that border bullring suggested he might have been en route to the Stellarmans' home county prior to that gundown.

But whither now, Charron?

His thoughts deepened.

Maybe that bullring episode had forced him to change his plans and hide out from the Federales in the Mexican sierras. A sensible man would surely react that way, but how had that slaughter man ever been?

'There you go again, Chance.'

'Huh?'

'Tell me you weren't brooding about Charron.'

'Honest, mother.'

She squeezed his hand and laughed. 'I'm only

pleased you're a better son than liar,' she said, and they continued on up to the house where Sherman stood waiting upon the main gallery with a whiskey glass in his hand.

He gave them a disapproving look. He always felt shut out whenever his wife and second youngest son were together. There was nothing he could do about it. Chance would always listen politely to any lecture he might deliver, then go ahead and do whatever he wanted anyway. And the cattleman had never been able to influence his wife, not even when she had shamed him before the whole country those long years ago.

'Waiting to join us for supper, Sherman?' Dyana smiled as they mounted the steps.

'Not exactly.' He took a swig of his whiskey, then fished something from a fob pocket. 'The jeweller's boy brought this . . . said you had it cleaned.'

It was a solid silver cross and chain, inscribed on the reverse side of the cross with the words: My dearest son. It was his mother's birth gift to him and he'd worn it all his life. The others all had them – Lafe, Travis and the late Carter. All pure silver and carrying the same loving inscription.

'I've also had Carter's crucifix polished and re-boxed recently.' Dyana's tone was soft. 'Don't you see, honey? That's why I don't want you going off doing anything foolish. Two sons I shall never see again. Surely that's enough for any mother?'

'Two? Oh, yeah . . . two.' Sometimes Chance tended to forget the long-dead boy Dyana had with *bandido* Antonio Villanova. 'How old would Richard be now, mother?'

They were climbing the steps to see the guests had assembled beyond the great double doors, chatting and laughing. Chance acknowledged them but his mother seem unaware of any of them at that moment.

'Twenty seven,' she said with that look she always had when talking of the brother they'd never seen. 'So beautiful and sweet – the image of his father. He was indeed my dearest son, then later you came along and took away the pain. God sent you to take his place.'

She would have said more, but Lafe appeared from inside, waving a letter. It was addressed to Chance, and the writer was Alma Mariano.

Chance scanned the note quickly, and then read it aloud to his family, their several guests and the mail-rider who'd brought it out from town.

Writing on the Don's behalf, Alma made it very clear that the rumors of Charron being still alive would not in any way affect the ongoing peace between the two cattle kingdoms. Her father, the Don, said he wished to make this eminently clear. Yet in the closing paragraph Alma had added – obviously without her father's knowledge – that she and her brothers and sisters were actually quite concerned about the situation. Back in the days when the Legend–Palo Pinto range war had raged most fiercely, Charron had fought with the Mexicans against Legend with bloody effect. The inference in

63

Alma's last paragraph was she feared that should Charron return to Palo Pinto, her volatile father might just be tempted to use the gunfighter to intimidate Legend in an attempt to again assume dominance of the cattle industry of the entire region.

The girl closed with a plea for Legend to send someone south to consult with her temperamental parent, and remind him forcibly that the feud genuinely was over and the fighting really was finished forever.

Later that night, the sober family members assembled in Stellarman's study to discuss Alma's request. Even a reluctant Dyana was eventually forced to agree that the man most suited to the task was Chance.

CHAPTER 5

WHO KILLED
THE GRINGO

Charron stood in the doorway of the workshop at the back of the funeral parlor, watching the crisp curls of wood shavings fall from the carpenter's plane. On a rough wooden bench close by, a gray sheet of canvas covered a figure. All that was to be seen of the dead man was a pair of scuffed and cracked range boots. Until the previous day those boots had supported a large and loud mouthed gringo named Buck Walker. Last night, somebody had blown Walker's face off in a back alley, and he was due to be laid to rest the following day – almost certainly with very few mourners in attendance.

Nobody knew who dispatched Buck Walker. None really cared. Had there been a peace officer here in Rio Alto, the death may have been investigated.

Then again, maybe not. Troublesome gringos were not highly regarded this side of the border.

Yet in recent times there had been a concerted attempt made to improve Mexico-US relations, and it was rumoured that the new governor would come to Rio Alto to show at least some official concern over the loss of an American citizen.

The governor would most likely simply make a few vague assurances of full investigations and retribution to appease any outraged feelings, then climb back aboard his luxury coach and leave the town to its heat-stricken squalor again.

The ancient carpenter worked dexterously, despite gnarled and rheumatic hands. Every so often he would glance across at the lean stranger in the doorway with a question in his eyes. He considered it sick and unwholesome the way some folks hung around funeral parlours, and he might have said as much – to just about any other man.

Not this one.

With a new growth of coal-black beard obscuring the lower half of his face, and with twin Colts buckled low and a black cheroot jutting from startlingly white teeth, Charron presented an intimidating sight that commanded respect wherever he might appear.

His luxurious whiskers had ensured his anonymity thus far. The hills and plains were crawling with *Rurales* and Federales out hunting the 'mad dog killer of Los Santos' these days, while the trees and marker posts of the countryside were sprinkled with recently printed actual photographs of the wanted matador-pistolero, which showed him clean-shaven, as recorded by the photographer at the bullring before that day exploded into utter chaos.

The gunman smiled, recalling Buck Walker and that hardcase's gross bad luck in recognizing him from the bullfight. Poor dumbass old Buck wouldn't be spilling his big secret to anyone here or anyplace else this side of Heaven now.

Ole, Charron! Hoofs, horns, tail to the Matador!

The ancient carpenter straightened from his task with a satisfied sigh. He looked at Charron who gave him a big bogus smile.

'You work well, old carpenter.'

'*Gracias.*'

Charron removed the stogie from his mouth. 'I always believe they should be covered over quickly before they begin to stink, don't you?'

Just the way he spoke threw a fresh scare into the old man. The carpenter worked in an atmosphere of death, yet always treated the departed with respect. There was no hint of respect in this black-bearded stranger's manner or voice. The man was trying to think of something to say when Charron flicked his still-smoking butt into a pile of shavings upon the floor, tapped his sombrero brim and disappeared.

The old man hastily dumped water upon the burning shavings and tried to remember if he had ever seen such cruelty in a man's eyes before. . . .

On the square, Charron gazed into the distance to see a cloud of dust billowing down the road from Palo Pinto. He stood motionless with a restless wind lifting the corners of his ornately worked serape. He remained well clear of the crowd gathering before the hotel to welcome the Don. He stood with one hip outthrust with all his weight upon the sound leg. He still limped slightly, but nowhere near as badly as when he had faced the bull at Los Santos.

His body was healing but his mind was something else again.

The handsome carriage rolled smoothly into the square and people leaned forward to get a look at the Don.

Four heavily armed outriders escorted Mariano's luxurious rig. Unrecognizable to the ranchero with his bristling black beard, Mexican disguise and concealed sixshooters, Charron's unblinking black eyes ran over the riders, weighing them up professionally. He was unimpressed. Yet he was impressed when the coach door opened and a tall and well-made man stepped on to the foot board, causing the coach to sag a little on that side.

Mariano had always been impressive. Born to riches, he was gifted with a natural grace and style reinforced by great arrogance. The big rancher's personal bodyguard, the massive Quintaro, was aging some but still looked as formidable a man as the killer had ever seen.

There was no love lost between Mariano and Charron these days. The killer had hired his gun to the big man during the range wars against the Stellarmans, had indeed been the Don's most dangerous weapon throughout that conflict. But they were too much alike to remain friendly in peace time. Charron respected the land-and-beef baron, but knew he would contract to kill him should someone want to pay him enough. Of course, to do that, he mused, he would first be obliged to eliminate Quintaro, the Don's lifelong bodyguard. He had no feelings about this seemingly indestructible giant of a man, while to Quintaro, Charron was simply a rabid dog.

The Don stepped down, resplendent in cloak and a tall hat with black feathers on the brim.

'Big man!' sneered Charron's mind. Yet his words seemed weak and almost envious. Following the range war the Don had continued to prosper, while Charron had damn near got himself killed half-a-dozen times since their last meeting. It didn't help any to see that Mariano appeared to be on top of the world right now, his manner maybe even a little condescending towards him when their glances finally locked. Deep down he was aware the Don had always intimidated him just a little with his inherited wealth and fine manners, yet he would drink quicklime before he would ever confess to such a thing.

Whatever or whoever Charron envied, he automatically also hated.

The killer sucked in a sharp intake of breath as the woman was handed down from the carriage. Alma Mariano was lovelier than ever in regal silk and snow-white lace.

The *pistolero* licked dry lips. He either genuinely loved this beautiful young woman or simply lusted after her; it didn't matter which. He wanted her the way a man dying of thirst craves a gallon jug of ice-cold beer.

His slender hands brushed the jutting butts of his Colt .45s in a gesture that reflected frustration, envy, anger and – rare for him – impotence.

This woman had always been aware of his feelings, but that meant nothing to her. She never gave him a second glance; she had only ever had eyes for Chance Stellarman – the snooty bitch!

But of course he would never give up on her. That was not his nature. When Stellarman was dead with six of his slugs in his guts, she would come to him readily enough. She would do so because he would make it plain that failure to do so would be tanta-mount to signing her own death warrant.

With love or lust, as with anything else he desired, he played the game hard.

The splendid party made its way across to the hotel where food and wine were elaborately laid out. This was an occasion of note arranged by the local cham-ber of commerce to celebrate and give thanks for the ongoing climate of peace existing between the once warring ranchers.

One extra black-bearded stranger swathed in an enveloping serape was neither here nor there in this crowd.

The refreshments were followed by speeches and toasts, after which the Don inspected a new public utility followed by a visit to the *teniente*, who gave him a sanitized account of the death of Buck Walker.

The eyes of rancher and killer met again at that point, without a flicker of recognition on Mariano's part. The Don represented the law here and had just learned that Walker had been gunned down by person or persons unknown. Charron smiled and lifted his glass to Mariano who continued calmly on to his next inspection, after which he took up a stand in the square and made a brief address.

'There exists now a new climate of harmony between our people and those north of the Rio Grande, my good and loyal citizens,' he told a motley collection of winos, wife-beaters, drunks, knife-artists, card cheats, percentage-girls, hookers and pimps mixed in with just a light sprinkling of decent folk who had made it to the cantina. 'As you may know, I have personally been responsible for more than one whole year of good relations with our former antagonists to the north, the Stellarman ranch.'

He paused for a light spatter of applause.

'As a result, we are all progressing with great success . . . and in time such regrettable incidents as befell Señor Walker shall become a thing of the past. And now it is my pleasure to invite you all to join me in the cantina – as my honored guests.'

They applauded the invitation with genuine enthusiasm. They didn't swallow all the big talk about peace and prosperity for a moment, and could care less about the dead gringo. But free liquor? They believed in that to a man.

It was a half hour later and the Don's entourage had

separated from the smelly herd and were now enjoying a fortifying drink at the quiet end of the barroom, when a shadow fell across the cantina's rear entrance.

Charron's abrupt appearance created a momentary hush. Even though only one or two at most figured who it might be behind that intimidating beard, there was more than enough about his style and general appearance to command full attention.

Still swathed in his serape, the killer approached the Don casually yet boldly. Alert as always, Quintaro checked out the newcomer with wise, sun-wrinkled eyes. The man's huge right hand rested on the butt of the long-barrelled revolver thrust through his six-inch belt. By this, every eye in the place was on the stranger with the beard.

Suddenly Quintaro stiffened. 'It is him!'

The Don turned casually, giving no hint of surprise. But Quintaro had his gun in hand by this, all of Mariano's entourage immediately following suit. Although it was a fact of life that this man had fought with the Palo Pinto against Legend Ranch in the past, much water had flown under the bridges since then. Yet the man in the serape appeared amiable enough, even managing a genial smile all round as he spread both empty hands in a peaceful gesture.

'*Amigos*,' he said. 'Peace be with you.'

Peace be with you? To some, this sounded almost more threatening than if he had come out shooting – Charron style.

'*Patron*,' he addressed Mariano. 'Surely this is not how you treat an old friend, and might I say – a friend who once saved your life?'

It was true. The killer had hauled Don Miguel from the jaws of a Legend ambush at Catfish Creek in New Mexico three years earlier. What could Mariano do now but nod, step forward and extend his hand.

'Welcome back, *pistolero*.'

The hand went unclaimed. Too many suspect people in a confined space for Charron to risk having someone grab his gun hand, if even for a moment.

'You look well, Don Miguel,' he said. He lifted his brows. 'We can talk?'

Although slightly uneasy, Miguel nodded and led the way to a far corner of the big room. Quintaro made to follow but Charron signalled him back with a stare as cold as death. Moments later he was smiling genially again as the two took chairs at a table and locked glances.

'You seem uneasy to see me, Don Miguel.'

'Not at all. You look well.'

'Of course you lie. I had a church fall upon me and a whole town try to murder me ... not to mention the bulls. But I improve by the day. So, I shall come to the point, Don Miguel. I offer my services.'

Mariano leaned back. 'What services?'

'*Señor*, I have but one great talent, if one overlooks the ring. I come to offer my gun, of course.'

'I appreciate your offer, but I have no use of a skill such as yours any longer. I am sure you have heard – the range war is over. We are at peace.'

'Peace? Now there you have a word whose meaning I never understood.'

It was difficult to tell if Charron was serious or not. Mariano wanted to remain distant and aloof, but curiosity got the better of him. 'That affair at Los Santos. The bullring? That was you, was it not?'

'Of course. Who else would dare?'

'You realize that as honorary governor I could have you arrested, tried and hanged?'

'No, you could not.'

'If Don Miguel says he can do a thing,' Quintaro interjected from the sidelines, 'then he can.'

Charron ignored the interruption. 'Two arguments against what you say, Don Miguel. One . . . before I hanged I would reveal all your evil doings during your wars with the Stellarmans . . . and then we might well hang side by side.'

'And the other?'

'Well, should you attempt to have me arrested here, I would first shoot you and your buffalo man here, and perhaps some of your flunkies and even some of the pigs posing as people in this place. There is surely no need to remind you that I can do all that I say, and even more?'

By this Don Mariano no longer looked like the man in charge. He was haggard and uneasy, while the whole now-silent room looked on.

'This is all foolish talk,' he said unevenly. 'For the

war with Legend is truly over.'

'Such things are never over until one side or the other claims victory. Your so-called truce with Stellarman has no chance of survival and shall last no longer than the day when those dogs believe you have let your guard down, then they will strike and destroy you. Only I can protect you. I can kill them all if you but meet my price and say the word.'

Miguel looked bemused.

'You know, gunfighter, I always suspected you hated the Stellarmans even more than I do myself. I can see today that this is so. What I do not understand, is why? What did they ever do to you to attract such ferocious hatred?'

The killer's face went blank. For a rare moment in his life, Charron seemed confused, unsure. For this was a question he had often asked himself over the years. Why Legend Ranch? He could not deny that he'd harboured a personal kind of hate towards the giant New Mexican outfit for as long as he could remember. Yet where this sprang from, and what kept it gnawing away at his guts, year in and year out, he was no closer to understanding than ever.

With a powerful act of will he forced himself to be calm.

'We stray from the point, Don Miguel. I offered to help you. Do you reject my offer?'

Don Miguel proved himself as apt at slipping back into character as the gunman.

'I do indeed,' he replied sternly, and rising sharply, turned and walked away.

Charron remained seated, staring blankly at the wall as he listened to the sounds the Palo Pinto party made getting up and quitting the building.

His features were expressionless, but that meant nothing. He reached for his cigarettes then went motionless at the sound of a woman's voice outside. A familiar voice.

Moving quickly to the open doors, he sighted her immediately standing there in the moonlight holding Mariano's hand in her own.

Alma.

The scatter of people in the yard went silent at sight of him, and the Marianos, father and daughter, turned together to see him coming down the steps.

He halted before them to sweep off his hat and bow low.

'Señorita Alma. Your servant.'

Alma shrank back, suddenly pale. She clutched her father's hand more tightly. Mariano moved forward protectively, his characteristic arrogance fully in evidence again now.

'I am afraid you alarm my daughter, Señor Charron. If you would be so good as to go—'

'Alarm?' Charron appeared pale. 'Alma, do I alarm you?'

'After what you did at Los Santos . . . you can ask me that?' the young woman retorted. 'All those people you hurt or killed . . . Father, surely you have not been speaking with this . . . this creature who should be in a cage?'

Charron dipped his head, tugging at his beard.

Although his posture did not appear to change, a terrible dejection seemed to transfix him.

It seemed that even if bullets and blades, the horns of great bulls and even collapsing churches could not really harm him, the scorn and contempt from this woman he believed he loved had the power to reduce him to nothing.

'I have come to offer my services once again to your father, *señorita*,' he stated almost humbly. 'And to you. Why do you spurn me?'

Her face was a study in disgust.

'I was reared to love God and fear the devil,' she hissed. 'And . . . and I believe you to be the devil's son!'

Charron took this with head slightly bowed, like a boxer listening as the referee in the prize ring proclaimed his adversary the winner. Without a word he turned and walked towards the surrounding darkness. His limp was very pronounced now, and the serape seemed to impede his lurching progress.

Somehow, despite the agonizing buzzing in his temples, he reached the horse. He was oblivious of the staring faces as he threw himself into the saddle and raked so hard with huge rowel spurs that he left twin trails of crimson along the animal's flanks.

The boiling dust of his going was a long time settling.

The rumor reached Legend Ranch Monday night, and Tuesday found Chance Stellarman crossing the Rio Grande and pushing southwards.

Riding across the red hills and the bleak dun plains, he by-passed the little villages and worn out *rancheros* alike.

About the only way to make a quick peso down here, he reflected as he crossed yet another dried-out creek bed, was to buckle on a gun if you were a man, or to go buy yourself a low-cut dress and go visit the cantinas if you were a woman.

The stark contrast between this land of poverty and the lush place that was his destination had never seemed more clearly marked. Yet he knew this was of no consequence today. There were far more real and urgent problems on his mind. Mainly there was the concern, bordering almost on fear, that he might reach Palo Pinto too late.

He shook his head in annoyance. It simply was not his nature to worry, yet he'd been doing little more ever since quitting the home acres.

He wondered if what they had heard about Charron was fact, or just another of those seemingly endless rumors or stories that seemed to swirl around that gunshark's every move.

The information was that the killer had been sighted in the Palo Pinto region. But maybe it was just that – a story. For all he really knew the gunman might have taken ship to Peru to shoot up the Incas.

His jaws worked under his bronzed skin as he topped out a red ridge and sighted the ugly outline of Armadillo in the distance.

Pull yourself together, Stellarman, he chided himself. If the rumor should prove to be true, that

78

Charron had visited with the Don, then it might not necessarily mean anything sinister. Back on Legend, some had worried it could mean the killer was fixing to ride for Palo Pinto again. But just as easily it could also mean the Don would keep his word about maintaining the truce, and the Charron visit might prove to mean nothing of importance at all.

By the time he was approaching Armadillo he was easy again in his mind, even if still aware of how disastrous it could prove for the entire region should the Marianos be planning to reopen hostilities.

But mostly it could prove fatal to himself and Alma. If the shooting war started again, she would have to stand by her family as he would to his own.

But why? clamoured the back of his mind. What would Mariano stand to gain by renewing the old conflict?

He couldn't name one damn thing.

It was his first visit to Armadillo, yet the place had a very familiar look – sun-washed adobe, dusty streets, stink, heat and restless noise.

Heavily laden burros plodded the streets, flogged without energy or enthusiasm by surly brown men who eyed the gringo horseman bleakly. Piano music drifted gaily from a cantina into a town that could never be really gay or anything approaching it. There were worn faces, weary faces, finished faces. Armadillo was dying. Eventually it would simply dry up and blow away on the desert wind . . . while men like the Don and the Stellarmans continued to dine royally off imported silver plates.

Maybe he might get to witness his generation rectifying some of these imbalances one day, Chance mused as he took his horse to the livery stables. If he survived, that was. He was thinking crazy, he told himself – like a man in urgent need of a stiff shot.

But he didn't get it.

Instead, on his way inside, he encountered a man he knew from farther west in the Crucifix Desert region. The fellow informed him that, just twenty four hours earlier in a town down south, he had seen Don Mariano and a bearded man who could have been Charron together in the same saloon.

Chance was back in the saddle within minutes, a solitary horseman kicking a yellow plume of dust into the sky.

CHAPTER 6

RINCONADA GUNDOWN

Charron was heading for Cibola, the closest place he'd ever known to a home town. Battered and isolated, the squalid village was incongruously set deep in the heart of lush ranges where some of the finest fighting bulls of the region were bred.

There had been a time years ago where the young Charron had known most of those fearsome animals personally, some even by name.

His roots, such as they were, lay here.

Memories crowded in as familiar trees rose on either side of the trail – he sniffed old scents long forgotten and saw himself the day he had first come here – all that long way down from the Rio Grande.

He'd never been much good at figures but calculated he must have been around eight or nine years old when he finally turned his back on the great river and the ancient ferryman to 'see the world'.

He laughed aloud. See the world? Cibola sure was not the world or anything like it. But it had been, and still was, a major center for the breeding of the fighting bulls and that had been the lure for that ragged-assed river kid so long ago. . . .

'Always, with you, the bulls.'

Old Eldio had tried to warn him. Had told him a thousand times to stick to the river and forget bull-fighting. And while he was at it, he could do himself a great deal of good by forgetting fighting in general. 'Always with you, the fighting. . . .'

He chuckled.

Of course the old geezer might have been right – sitting back there on his battered old boat waiting to ferry travellers across the Rio Grande. Fighting either men or bulls was a good way to die young, although in his case he had prospered. Maybe that was because he eventually became so good at both forms of fighting.

He stroked his clean-shaven jaw. He'd felt the need to disguise himself for a spell in the aftermath of the Los Santos dust-up.

He grinned. For days following the bloodshed in the arena, the valleys and plains had been bristling with possemen hunting for that limping bullfighter who'd shot the bull then turned his smoking guns on the crowd. Of course, they'd had no hope of catching him. And even had they done so there would simply have been more corpses to bury.

The smile faded as he massaged the back of his neck. He had not one regret about the bloodbath in the stadium of the bulls. But he did brood regarding his poor performance in the ring that day. For he'd always been naturally brilliant against the bulls . . . always from the very start . . . here, where it all began. . . .

The bull's sharp hoofs ripped the soft earth as it charged, sending up dust and chunks of ripped grass behind its muscular hindquarters as it flung its enraged mass towards its tormentor like a freight loco on legs.

The boy stood gracefully, fearlessly in its path, armed only with a flutter of grubby red rags fastened upon a sharp stick. A strip of the same material was tangled about the bull's left horn. This was not its first charge. Indeed, the very way in which the whole area of the back pasture was torn and ploughed up showed just how long the illicit 'bullfight' had been in progress.

Although the beast had swept frighteningly close to its tormentor on many occasions, it had not succeeded in touching him even once.

Back on the Rio Grande the ragged kid had picked fights with cattle, horses, savage dogs and sometimes drunken citizens – anything that would provide him with the opportunity to practise his ducking, weaving, jabbing with his stick and, most important of all, surviving.

The bull was desperately close, eyes red with rage,

slobber streaming from its jaws.

Yet again, the ragged boy raised his banner of rags, or muleta as he chose to call it, subtly fluttering the corners to divert the beast's attention from his motionless body, allowing the animal to follow the lure past him before suddenly jerking it high, by which stratagem he brought the animal to a bewildered halt, leaving him standing there, calm and unscathed.

'Charron!' chorused the excited brats perched atop the highest rail out of harm's way. Then: 'Bravo! Bravo! Bravo!'

They knew their bullfighting, these ragged street urchins of Cibola. They knew all the matadors who visited the town by name, and they attended every corrida held here as favor-sellers, messengers and general roustabouts. . . .

The memories faded as the killer rode past the sign that read CIBOLA 3 MILES. He was boosted by all the great memories and the sights and sounds of this old hell-hole town he was approaching . . . and so didn't get to see them, at first.

They appeared as twin specks in the far distance behind. Gradually the dots in the sky grew bigger to eventually reveal themselves, firstly as birds, then large birds, and finally birds of prey.

The giant Sonoran buzzards of the region were grotesque and would frighten most anybody, yet scarcely terrify. It would seem abnormal for a grown man, in particular a professional man-killer and bullfighter, to whip his horse under the cover of the trees at sight of the creatures then haul his serape over his head and shoulders and cower there after the devil birds were long gone.

When he emerged from cover it took several minutes before he was composed enough to continue on his way, eyes still searching the now empty skies. Eventually he was sitting his mount straight-backed and arrogant again with one hand on gunbutt, ready in the event somebody might have witnessed his strange behaviour and should prove fool enough to comment.

When he felt normal again he took to conjuring up those familiar sights and sounds of the long ago. . . .

Memories cleared like shifting clouds and he lifted his head proudly. It seemed he could still hear the chanting: 'Charron! Charron! Charron!' A sneer rode his mind. They had idolized him but in the end all had failed him in one way or another, turning against him as people had been doing all his life.

But his thoughts were turning darker again as he rode through the dusk down a twisted street past a battered town sign. He knew the buzzards were responsible for the mood coming over him. Such incidents, dating back as far as memory reached, invariably left him edgy and unsure. Whenever he felt that way, the only one way he knew to claw his way back and recover his powers lay in violence or cruelty which reassured him that a man afraid of birds could still be very much a man.

A passing mule driver stared at this handsome

stranger. He saw a young man with old eyes who rode lightly in the saddle. The driver, struck by the sheer intensity of his stare as Charron passed him by, reined in and looked after him. The man felt he detected something familiar about the stranger. But too many years had elapsed since he'd been a skinny kid perched atop a fence in the moonlight, shouting, 'Charron! Charron!' as his friend risked his life in an enclosure with a giant fighting bull below.

Much blood had flowed since Charron had outgrown Cibola.

The sun disappeared and the horse arched its neck in a sudden toss as Charron rode on past the church.

His lip curled in contempt. From his earliest days he had hated religion and all things religious. The irony in this was that the single item he'd ever owned, dating back to when he had one day mysteriously appeared alone, starved, bloodied by wild birds and terrified – from out of noplace at an ancient ferryman's riverside shack by the Rio Grande – happened to be a religious icon.

He reached inside his shirt and drew out the crucifix on its silver chain.

Most times it made him feel good to simply touch the object and reflect on it. Not tonight. The devil birds had unbalanced him and he had that old creeping sensation that if he didn't take a powerful drink very soon some nameless disaster would strike.

He always spat whenever he passed a church. He did so now, and it cheered him some. A pious old crone selling her beads upon the low church wall clucked in disapproval but he did not even hear.

Now the demons were completely closing him in. In the darkening wells of his brain he felt that great changes were at hand, that his destiny was about to redefine itself in some significant way.

But whether that change might lead him to the stars or the pits of hell, there was no guessing.

Times like this, the Matador was as much a mystery to himself as to others.

Approaching the cantina, he glimpsed a voluptuous young woman he imagined resembled Alma Mariano. A nerve in his cheek began to twitch. He clamped his jaws tightly and brought the horse in neatly to the hitch rail.

The Marianos! How he hated them all. The Marianos and the Stellarmans both. From earliest memory he had reacted violently against both great spreads and their people, had fought both with and against the Marianos and had once slain a Stellarman. He knew he would never be free of those hatreds which he seemed to have been born with, and which were growing infinitely more intense in recent times.

When he dismounted he willed away any suggestion of a lingering limp, closing his mind to the pain in his knee.

Yet the injury was improving by the day. He thought of those who had shouted 'El rengo!' that day at Los Santos, and laughed softly. Many of them were not shouting tonight, but howling in the black bowels of hell.

He entered the smoke-filled room and nobody recognized him. As far as this place knew, he was a total stranger here. But because he was the one revisiting his roots, he was on the lookout for the familiar, and here and there glimpsed a look, a gesture, even one face that he surely recalled from the old days.

But the place itself had changed. Back then it had been a cesspit. Over the years it had prospered however, was now the prime watering place within twenty miles. It had acquired a rough and ready status and was frequented by patrons who could afford the higher prices which deterred the riff-raff. He saw big men in flashy shirts and tied-down revolvers gliding across the tiny dance floor with women who painted their faces.

Outlaws.

Charron recognized the breed on sight. It seemed curious, yet finding himself surrounded by his own dangerous kind made him feel almost at home, something the old town itself had failed to do.

He encouraged dark memories as he sought a quieter corner of the bar and signalled for a shot. He had begged for centavos in this place, run messages for drunks and had been kicked, cussed and abused for his reward.

And Alma Mariano had insulted him! whispered the back of his mind.

The thought startled him. Now, where had that unwelcome thought sprung from. That silver-tailed bitch had no business intruding upon him here!

He suddenly laughed out loud and tasted his tequila. When he shut his eyes he found he could no longer see the devil birds. Charron was whole and strong again. Bravo!

'*Hombre?*'

She was pale and petite, and almost lovely, for a cheap cantina hustler. She smiled up at him with red lips and rested a familiar hand upon his shoulder.

'You buy me a drink, stranger?'

'Go away, little slut.'

His voice was soft, one rub above a whisper. Yet it brought flames to her cheeks. She might be a whore, but she was a proud whore. She called him an ugly name then flounced back to the companions whom she had deserted for what she had mistaken for a client.

Charron smiled at his handsome image in the dark bar mirror. The tequila was starting to hit. Then the bar man loomed before him, a face from the past.

'Do I not know you, *señor?*'

'No.'

'You are sure?'

'Go clean your spittoons.'

The man flushed but moved away without comment, glancing back over his shoulder.

A second double and he was shrugging off his earlier low mood. He would have her eventually. Alma. He always got what he wanted. When she finally became his own, he might hang up his guns and stop butchering people like culled cattle. The

Don could write him a full full pardon then give him his daughter's hand in marriage. He would dress with silk next to his skin and learn what wine went with what food.

Who could tell? Maybe one day he would even get to figure out why he had been so long obsessed with Legend Ranch and the people on it. Time, someone had said, would eventually unravel all mysteries.

'*Hombre*! You insult my woman!'

Charron looked at him without interest. One of the flashy dancers. Big and flushed with booze. Strong as a working bullock. But what did that count? Everybody was a midget alongside a man with a gun – and he was the man with the gun.

He looked beyond the heavyweight to see the pretty little whore. She stood with his henchmen with hands on hips and looking very pleased with herself.

'Your woman,' he said with slow deliberation, 'is indeed a whore. She was born a whore, has lived all her life as a whore, and will one day die—'

He broke off and bobbed low as a ham-sized fist whistled over his head. Charron's eyes lighted. Until that moment he'd been unsure what was missing. Now he knew. Action and excitement, the eternal life-savers.

He evaded the next punch with ridiculous ease and broke the man's nose with a sideways chop of his hand. Blood splashed red under the lights and the man bent forward to avoid splashing his shirt front with blood. Charron's knee whipped upwards into the unprotected face, sending the fellow reeling across the little dance floor with his face all off-center and crimson running from nose, ears and mouth, choking on his own blood.

They came at him in a rush as he knew they would.

The leader clawed for a heavy old-fashioned revolver thrust through his stylish cummerbund. To everyone else, it appeared he drew his piece with commendable speed and skill.

Not to the Matador.

Charron had seen quicker snails.

At last the old gun was fully clear of the cummerbund. Charron watched the wicked black muzzle rising, winking beneath the lamplight. All around the room, customers huddled together waiting for the inevitable and wondering why the stranger did not at least attempt to defend himself against Big Lupe.

Then Charron drew.

He shot the man squarely between the eyes and he fell slowly backwards with his sixgun still unfired locked in his frozen fist.

The hardcases should have let it go at that. Instead, they found confidence from their numbers, and clawed for their weapons.

There was a great singing in Charron's skull as he went low and drilled the nearest man through the belly. Instantly he lifted his sights and blasted out an overhead light, sprang nimbly to one side and killed two more with two bullets.

For the disbelieving onlookers it was like watching men mired in mud trying to deal with a whirling dervish.

Spinning, ducking and dancing, Charron kept shooting and killing. And when his Colt ran empty he snatched out its companion piece and shot another two down before ducking behind the bar.

He was heading for the batwings in a low crouch when he sighted the girl through the gunsmoke. She was running up the stairs. He triggered from the hip. The girl staggered up three more steps, froze, stretched both arms wide and fell slowly backwards.

Then the Matador was gone.

He hit the saddle with but one light bullet graze on the left forearm to show for all the murderous gunplay.

He was out of the lamplit square within seconds. Soon he was gone from Cibola.

Horse stretching out underneath him and the blood pounding in his veins from the excitement, Charron rode the dark night trail like a king.

All uncertainty was now gone, all his ghosts laid to rest. He'd arrived at that dirty little town darkly brooding about birds. Yet the simple 'cure' of shooting up an entire saloon and leaving behind death and terror had purged him of his weaknesses.

Glancing back from the flank of a high rise, he saw smoke and flame belching into the night sky over his old home town.

That was his salute to the past and testimony to what lay ahead.

It was all so clear now. Whatever demons drove him and fired his restless spirit he'd never understood. Yet he did know now that whatever his destiny might be, it surely lay back east – back where the great ranches had warred, made peace, and now must fight once more. He would have the Spanish woman, he promised himself. In time he would see Legend Ranch in ashes for all the hurt they had caused him. The future was visible in startling clarity – chaos, death, destruction – with Charron stoking the furnaces.

Legend Ranch had always been the only enemy ever to defeat him. He would concede that now. But soon they would become as nothing, their sons dead in the earth, their pride and vanity blown away along with their riches, like dust.

Legend first, he promised himself – then Palo Pinto.

That starving orphaned brat with no name running through the night from a terror of cruel birds, had grown into a proud man of the gun – yet was still to be spurned for what he was ... would from this day on avenge every hurt in blood. And a proud aristocratic woman would know her only salvation was Charron's mercy.

And for that, Alma Mariano would have to beg.

Chance and Alma passed through Don Miguel's ornate iron gates and strolled arm in arm along the flagged path winding through the gardens. There was a scent of roses and honeysuckle in the night, and the evening air ruffled the ornamental trees and shrubs with a whispering softness.

93

They walked in silence for a piece, her lovely face turned up to his.

'You are very quiet tonight, Chance.'

'Sorry. Still a little tired from the ride, I guess.'

'Yet you were not weary yesterday when you arrived.'

'I wasn't?'

'You know you were not.'

They halted before the long, pillared portico. Alma lifted her heavy black hair from the back of her neck and let the cool wind touch her skin.

'I know why you are quiet tonight, Chance. It is because of that news from Cibola.'

'Why should that bother me?'

'Because you believe the man who killed all those people was Charron.'

He frowned at her. 'I didn't say that.'

'Nobody did. But I know that the Don, Quintaro and my brother Joachim all believe it, also.' Her lovely mouth twisted. 'Nobody kills like Charron. We all know that.'

He couldn't deny it. His discussions with the Don and his sons had progressed well enough. Joachim, Francisco and Simon had seemed at least halfway convincing when they spoke of continuing harmony between the spreads. The Don said much the same thing, yet Chance found him less convincing.

Mariano did not trust him. Nor did he trust Legend. Their ongoing relationship would be a chancy thing at best until Don Miguel fully accepted their protestations of goodwill.

Then came the news from Cibola.

The first stark report was that a stranger had gone loco with his guns and many people had died. Nobody had mentioned Charron's name, but after later receiving a description of the killer the Palo Pinto was convinced it had been Charron the mad killer. It seemed unlikely that there could be more than one man in all Mexico capable of such senseless slaughter.

Chance and Joachim had immediately made their plans in the wake of the incident. If Charron was on a killing spree it stood to reason that he might well strike out against the Palo Pinto, Legend, or both. He had done so before, and who could know what a mad dog killer might do next?

It was quickly decided that rather than wait for that to happen, Charron should be hunted down now and dealt with while they still had some notion where they might look for him.

Chance was not ready to take a guess on that. Hauling out an old map, he studied the region surrounding Cibola in ever widening circles until his eye lit upon a name.

Rinconada.

He leaned back and thoughtfully massaged his jaw.

Rinconada was a remote outpost far beyond the reach of the law, he knew. It was also known far and wide as a hellion's roost where that breed felt free to hole up with women, wine and cards to while away his leisure hours . . . and no law within fifty miles.

Charron had just killed in Cibola.

It seemed to add up that a place like Rinconada would seem an inviting destination where a man on a murder spree might get to rest up with his own kind and not fear waking up one morning with a marshal's shotgun resting against his temple.

When he informed the others of his thoughts, a drinker overheard and insisted he'd often heard that Rinconada was actually an old stamping ground of Charron's. That decided it.

Suddenly all three felt a great urgency to act and not simply sit back waiting to see where the mad dog might strike next.

'Go carefully, my caballero,' Alma pleaded later as they made their goodbyes. She smiled. 'I do not wish to lose you even before we reach the altar.'

'I'm a hard man to lose, Alma. *Adios*, Don Miguel.'

There was no response from the tall man standing by the gates. As always, Don Mariano was uneasy with anything involving Legend Ranch. Indeed he'd attempted to dissuade his bodyguard and his son from accompanying Stellarman, but he'd been over-ridden.

Chance's lips were still tingling from Alma's kiss as he rode off with Joachim Mariano and the giant Quintaro. After a time he glanced back to see a flutter of white lace from an upstairs window. He returned the wave and winked at Joachim.

'A special woman, your sister, Joachim.'

'She has a brain,' the young man said soberly. 'Which is more than could be said of all Marianos at times.'

'What do you mean?'

Joachim shrugged. 'I talked with the Don after supper. Ahhh, Chance, those fathers of ours are like old range bulls who have ruled over all they survey for far too long. It is hard to change their ways, shed their old suspicions. . . .'

'Suspicions?'

Joachim shrugged. 'We all know you came down here simply to help ensure there might be no more fighting between the ranchos, *amigo*. But the Don, of course, is still full of suspicions, while your father can still be difficult. As I say, like two old range bulls. . . .'

They rode for a time in silence.

Then Chance said, 'You don't expect troubles to break out between the ranches again, do you?'

'I shall not allow it,' the other replied. Joachim squared his shoulders. 'The Don grows older every day while I grow stronger.' He paused to grin. 'But if he tries to ride roughshod over me, I've always got Quintaro here to lean on. Is that not so, big one?'

The largest man on Palo Pinto, looking like some ancient hero of legend astride his huge mount, nodded his grizzled head.

'The peace must be kept,' he said in his direct way, eyes probing every shadow, tree, bush and hollow as they rode. 'Even if it means me taking the great Don aside and telling him so.'

Reassured, Chance rode on ahead for several hours until the lights of Rinconada flickered in the darkness ahead.

The trio set out to do the rounds of the cantinas

and low dives over the next couple of hours. They quizzed the locals and made no secret of the fact they were searching for Charron. This was undeniably a cutthroat outlaw town yet Charron boasted no friends here. Shooting gunmen and rich men for money was one thing. But mass slaughter was surely something else. In Rinconada, the term 'mad dog' was to be heard whenever the topic turned to the Matador that night.

Midnight found the three sinking their final tequila in the quietest cantina before turning in. They had known from the outset it would be a long shot, coming here. They'd not picked up a single lead clue on the gunman's whereabouts, which gave rise to a slender hope he may have been wounded in Cibola and had possibly perished. It was a slim hope but one worth clinging to. It was all they had.

It was cold as they crossed the empty plaza on their way to the livery stables. A stiff wind coming in off the plains caused the old bells in the church's skinny steeple to murmur softly in the night. A yellow hound with a lame leg limped by and vanished down an alley searching for something to eat – anything to eat.

The town was quiet as a grave until they reached the livery where they were met in the doorway by a man with eyes the size of saucers. He was fearful and sweating.

'Señor Joachim – *amigos*,' he panted, gesturing wildly in the lamplight. 'I have been waiting for you to return.' His eyes rolled. 'He is here!'

'Who?' Chance said sharply. Then his eyes snapped wide. Charron?'

The liveryman reached out shakily to seize Joachim by the arm. 'The evil one is here! Just a little time ago, I go along to the old mission yonder where I tether my mules for the grasses and—'

'Quickly, *señor*!' Joachim interrupted. 'Are you saying he's over at the mission?'

'*Sí*!' The fellow made the sign of the Cross on his bony chest before continuing. 'As plain as I see you . . . there he was, watering his horse and setting up camp. And, *señors*, I must tell you he was unsteady . . . indeed I believe the evil one is either wounded or drunk!'

He would have said more but suddenly found himself alone. Moving to the door which stood propped open to the night, he watched the three hurrying for the mission building.

The liveryman sagged against the doorframe, and there were tears in his eyes as he looked skywards. His lips trembled.

'Forgive me, Holy Virgin . . . but what else could I do. The evil Charron promised to kill me if I did not say what he said I must. . . .'

The ancient mission building was suffering the fate of all neglected adobe – the clay returning to the earth from which it came.

Rinconada had first seen life as a mission town back in the days when men believed in God and before the missionaries quit and their places were taken over by vermin posing as men.

For generations now, the cloisters of the chapels had sounded only to the occasional drunken voice of the derelict, or the cooing of the pigeons which fouled its once pristine walls.

Charron waited comfortably, ready to kill again.

From concealment he could clearly see three stealthy figures stalking warily towards where they believed he had made camp.

He had sighted the trio from concealment the hour they rode in, had been preparing ever since.

He noted with a professional eye that they were entering the campground exactly as he would have done, making full use of the cover and raising not a whisper of sound that might awake a sleeping killer.

He smiled and settled deeper into his blind.

He tried to force himself to calmness but it was impossible to contain his excitement.

A Mariano, Quintaro, and a Stellarman! Who could be calm with such a huge prize to be claimed?

The entire area was a wide open space surrounded on one side by ruins. The killer had taken time formulating his plans until convincing himself they were virtually fool proof.

He now stood in a shadowed alcove to the left of his stake out. When the shooting began, a survivor would have but one place to run here – back to the shadowed doorway some hundred feet from Charron's position – which Charron himself could reach unseen behind the cover of a broken wall.

What he planned was highly dangerous . . . yet

most of his life had been exactly that. . . .

He was a hundred feet from the small fire he had lighted over in the wide courtyard. There was no horse visible over there, just the little blaze and what appeared to be the figure of a sleeper huddled in his blankets.

Charron did not seem to breathe as the unmistakable silhouette of Quintaro drew level with his position. The big man paused, sniffing the air. He then moved on, a revolver in either massive paw.

From concealment, the unsuspected killer's eyes cut left.

Chance Stellarman and Joachim Mariano were passing a crumbling shrine to the Virgin. Their attention now was fully focused upon that realistic effigy of a sleeping person close to the fire.

They were very professional, the killer noted with a mocking smirk. What a pity he must slaughter such courageous ones!

His brain hummed with excitement. The Don's beloved son and his lifelong liegeman obviously slaughtered in cold blood by a Stellarman!

Such a happening could have but one possible result; Mariano rage and massive retaliation which could well result in Charron's lifetime dream coming to fruition – range war as never seen here before with his enemies tearing one another to pieces!

And he the chess master who would play out this titanic end game!

The gun-bristling trio were well beyond his concealed position by this, all with their backs to him.

It was time.

The moon shimmered down and the stalkers moved as silently as ghosts.

The wind creaked an open door. The little fire popped once – and Charron's guns opened up with a demonic thunder burst of sound that seemed to shake the world.

Quintaro first.

The giant took four bullets in the back before he could even cry out, before he could even begin to turn. A lesser man would surely have fallen down dead, yet Quintaro still stood clutching both revolvers as he jerked around to face his attacker, moving stiffly like the world's biggest puppet.

The killer ignored him.

He would waste no bullets on a dead man.

Instead in an instant he flicked smoking barrels to lock in on the slender figure of Joachim Mariano. The Don's eldest son died instantly as bullets exploded in his chest and ripped him apart.

It all occupied but seconds. Quintaro's dying came with a final mighty exhalation of breath, and Mariano was a lifeless shape draped across a blood-spattered chunk of old masonry as the murdering guns searched for their third and final target.

But Chance Stellarman was already halfway to the shadowed doorway, covering distance in giant strides and blasting in the direction the ambush shots had come from.

And the killer rushed equally swiftly to the same cover, which he reached with bare seconds to spare before Stellarman came diving through from the adjacent entrance way.

There was a moment when Chance was unsighted coming from moonlight into shadow, when he was diving full length in desperation before the ambush guns could find him also.

In that vital second Charron brought his upraised revolver smashing down to the back of the head. The second brutal blow would insure that he remained unconscious until the killer's plan had reached the next phase of the larger plan he'd conceived right at the last moment. Instead of killing all three, he envisioned a way whereby he could turn tonight into a final murderous war between his hated Rico enemies, Legend and Palo Pinto!

He had it in his power to engineer their destruction – if he played his cards right!

By this the whole town was awake with people pouring into the streets two hundred yards from the murder scene.

The killer was invisible behind cover, just a phantom voice in the night as he bawled at the top of his lungs, 'Murder! Murder! Chance Stellarman's killed them both! Stop him before he gets away! Look! There he goes – over yonder by that oak. Move, damn you, move!'

He was long gone before the first jittery towners showed up at the murder scene, toting their torches and lanterns.

The Rinconadans found two men dead, both Mexicans, each man riddled with lead and with his guns unfired. They also found one gringo very much alive, if badly shocked.

Of Charron there was no sign.

CHAPTER 7

THE DOGS OF WAR

Alma Mariano was past weeping and long beyond pleading. There was no indication amongst any of the grim-faced men gathered in her father's study that they might have heard one single word of her passionate entreaty.

Now a full council of war was underway.

The Don presided with his surviving sons, Simon and Francisco flanking his chair. Gathered in a somber semi-circle before the Marianos were fifteen men – hard, lean-bodied and silently grim every one. Palo Pinto's fighting elite had believed they had fought their last battle against Legend Ranch, until today. Now, in the wake of the double murder by a Stellarman, there had been no talk of peace between former enemies, only of war.

Directly beneath the plush chamber where they were assembled, Chance Stellarman sat lashed to a stout chair and under lock and key – already accused, tried and convicted of double murder in the minds of Legend's old enemies.

His face was battered and his body viciously bruised. The enraged citizenry of Rinconada had shown him no mercy, had paid not the slightest attention to his protestations of innocence as they'd trussed him up and dispatched a messenger to ride down to the Palo Pinto with news of the great tragedy.

He'd expected Don Mariano would shoot him then and there when he reached the rancho with the dead men. His son had restrained him. But he had been assured of a public hanging after Palo Pinto had 'dealt with' Legend.

The dogs of war were running wild and slavering on the Palo Pinto tonight. Chance was angry and dismayed by this turn of events yet the circumstantial evidence must appear compellingly overwhelming to a grieving and suspicious father.

The 'facts' – as viewed by hostile judges – could be seen as damning.

Chance had visited Rinconada with the Don's son and his bodyguard. A gun battle had erupted in which son and bodyguard perished while Chance survived almost without a scratch. Chance had counter-claimed Charron must have been in Rinconada and had ambushed them and slain his companions. Nobody in Rinconada could be found who could support his story, the one man who might have done so, the Rinconada liveryman, had taken flight and vanished.

The Palo Pinto's reaction to the tragedy had been inevitable and violent, he could see. A weeping Alma knew Chance to be innocent, but Don Mariano was not about to listen to any foolish daughter plainly blinded by love. He'd just lost a son and a lifetime friend, so it followed that the man responsible would pay the supreme penalty as would all Legend Ranch.

The Don believed he understood exactly what had taken place in Rinconada. Chance Stellarman, for evil reasons of his own, had lured Joachim and Quintaro to the helltown and its ancient mission with the intention of murdering them, after having set up the fake campsite to convince the Palo Pinto men they would find Charron there. How they'd come to find Chance battered unconscious at the murder scene was not explained, but certainly was none of Mariano's concern. It was sufficient for him that destiny had delivered his son's killer into his hands.

Chance's execution would appease some of the Don's wrath. But not all. Not nearly all.

The lengthy neutrality with the Stellarmans had been brutally blown to pieces by the murderous incident. There could be but one result.

War.

The great ranches had fought before, but this would be the final battle of destruction.

'I want every man present mounted, armed and ready to ride instantly,' the Don told his grim-faced audience at the conclusion of the council of war. 'And before we cross the Rio Grande I shall expect each one of you to swear a holy oath that he shall not return to Mexico until every last man bearing the accursed Stellarman name is in his grave!'

It was dawn before the last heavily armed vaqueros stormed from the ranch yard to gallop off in the wake of the ranch crew heading north.

Alma's exit from the huge front room where the women wept and prayed, went unnoticed. In the passageway she encountered a servant who shouted, 'Death to all Stellarmans!' causing her to start nervously.

All males here supported the Don's reactions to a man. But not this woman. Any of the women for that matter. They had had enough of range wars years ago.

Hurrying through the long corridors before making her swift way down flights of stairs, Alma knew her father would never forgive her in a lifetime for what she was about to do.

But she would still do it.

Two innocent men had already died in Rinconada, one a beloved brother. She would not allow the man she loved and believed in share the same fate at the hands of her father's riflemen.

She must set Chance free. She would!

Yet the moment she reached the underground cellars where he was being held, her courage almost evaporated.

Somehow she recovered, yet despite her commitment to what she must do, the girl could not suppress sickening feelings of guilt as she laced the wine with sleeping powder in the mansion's great tiled kitchen. She was forced to turn away in something like shame when young Mario Chanez thanked her warmly for fetching him a refreshing glass, which he immediately began sipping at his post outside the cellar door.

But she was all steely determination and commitment again by the time the young man slumped to the floor, was cool efficiency itself as she cut Chance loose and smuggled him safely outside to a waiting horse.

They barely spoke before he rode off; it seemed the disasters piling in upon them almost made speech all but impossible. But their long, last embrace said everything their lips could not.

Then he was gone.

Chance was fired upon twice before bursting clear of Palo Pinto's acres. He was unhurt, and with a sound horse under him, set a dead north course.

By this time he believed he understood the events that had overtaken him at Rinconada. Charron had cleverly set out to stage manage a situation in which two Palo Pinto men were murdered and himself deliberately left alive without witnesses – which could only be interpreted one way: the man responsible for the cold-blooded slaughter of two former foes was a former bitter Mariano enemy – Chance Stellarman.

Cold logic told him that Charron's sole motivation in staging that gruesome situation could only be to revive the war between the giant spreads and bring about their final destruction.

This Texan must get home, fast!

Charron leaned against his horse's shoulder, Mexican stogie between his teeth, smiling hugely like the cat that ate the cream.

It was chilly up here along the mesa trail south of the Rio, yet his shirt was opened to the waist as though in defiance of the elements.

Distant sounds reached him faintly as he took the cigar from between his perfect teeth. Raising his binoculars he was quick to pick out, what at a distance resembled a moving section of trail in the far distance, yet which he expected to eventually materialize into a virtual army on horseback heading north for the Rio Grande and Legend Ranch.

And it did.

It took the better part of an hour for the final straggler to pass by far below, by which time the killer's iron constitution was beginning to show signs of exhaustion. He attempted to estimate how long since he'd slept, but failed. But in general terms, he knew it to be over three days and nights – reaching back all the way to the day he'd ridden into the old home town to even a few scores.

This man needed to rest before joining in the 'final drama' that would soon be unfolding across the Rio Grande in old Texas. . . .

He slept in a leafy bower and had no notion how long he'd been there – certainly some hours – before aroused by the faint drumbeat of hoofs.

It took time to clamber back up to his lookout position where he was just in time to glimpse the speck of a horseman disappearing far up along the Rio Grande trail.

Stellarman!

For a long minute his rage got the better of him and he was virtually slavering before he finally brought himself under control.

He had no notion how the man had escaped from Palo Pinto, only knew he had no hope of running him down on a played-out horse.

He could live with that he assured himself, once back in the saddle with rage giving way to a cold, cruel calm now. The end result would be the same. For if Stellarman hadn't died at Palo Pinto he would surely perish in the conflagration about to consume both great *ranchos*.

All his hatred and cunning had gone into this – the final solution and day of retribution.

He considered himself now to have risen above petty personal feuds to achieve the lofty status of the commander in chief overviewing the staging of an historic battle of his own making. Individuals such as Chance Stellarman or Don Mariano were now seen from the heights of his obsession as mere chessboard pieces being guided to their destruction by his hand.

When the smokes of battle had finally cleared he knew they must proclaim: Charron rules!

And for just a moment out of time he allowed himself to ponder the great mystery of his life. Namely, the reason behind his obsession with the two

111

giants of the region. From his earliest remembrances he had been fascinated by both Palo Pinto and Legend, had many times aligned himself with the former and attacked the latter – while inwardly hating both equally.

He had spilled blood on both sides of that long-running feud and had always survived – believing he was destined to do so in order that, before his time came, he would see both giants dead and destroyed within the smoking ruins of their great empires.

Ole, Charron!

He swung into the saddle and set a leisurely pace northwards, his thoughts carrying him lightly across the miles. There was so much about himself and his destiny which he did not yet understand, and might never know. The one thing of which he was certain however, was the total conviction that when both Marianos and the Stellarmans had finished destroying one another, he would finally be free for the first time in his life.

His horse grunted in protest as he kicked it into a trot.

Chance could scarce find the strength to tumble from the saddle when he galloped into the headquarters. Stable hands came rushing out to help him down, but he brushed them roughly aside.

'See to the horse and call up my brothers,' he panted. 'There's big trouble on the way from the south and—'

'Oh, Chance, Chance, thank God you're here!' a

voice cried, and he swung to see Melanie rushing into the stables. She seized his arm and began dragging him toward the doors. 'Come quickly, you must—'

'Mel,' he said, resisting, 'there's one hell of a crisis and—'

'Of course there's a crisis! Mother has taken ill . . . or gone crazy or something!'

'Mother?'

In a the space of a heartbeat he'd whirled away and was running towards the house.

He was relieved to find Dyana seated in her favorite chair by the windows of her morning room, when he burst in with his sister at his heels. But when the woman turned to face him he realized something was seriously wrong. She appeared drugged or mentally affected, he wasn't sure which.

'Who is it?'

Dyana was staring directly at him but his face didn't seem to register. He rushed to her and drew her to her feet and wrapped his arms around her, protecting her, willing his strength into her. She shuddered and then looked up at him, her eyes beginning to clear. 'Chance . . . where have you been?'

'Thank God!' Melanie said fervently. 'We think she's been in shock and hasn't been herself ever since she saw this, Chance.'

The girl had gathered up a newspaper from a couch and held it up for him to see. Despite his preoccupation with his mother, Chance was startled to see the grainy photograph commanding the front page with the bold word KILLER! emblazoned above it.

There was no possible mistaking who it was. He was staring at the handsome arrogant face of Charron the Matador!

A subsequent quick scan of the article revealed that the photograph accompanied an article on the slaughter in the bullring of Los Santos some six weeks earlier. The picture was accredited to a Los Santos photographer and was an enlargement of a group picture of several 'tyros' taken that violent day by the same man.

It was an excellent likeness, most likely the first actual picture of the killer he'd ever seen.

When he looked a question at the two women, his sister said, 'Tell him, mother.'

'It's Antonio,' Dyana said. 'You know . . . Antonio Villanova?'

He looked blank. His mother still appeared quite strange, yet seemed now to be emerging from some kind of depression, or mental fog. He cursed the circumstances responsible for his lengthy absence.

He then focused on the name 'Antonio Villanova'. It seemed to ring a distant bell yet he still failed to understand why.

'You must remember . . . the man I ran off with, Chance! Antonio Villanova. The outlaw!'

Now he remembered! He had not been born when that great scandal rocked Legend Ranch, yet from time to time it was still resurrected here as a strange and dramatic saga from the Stellarman histories.

But he had no time for ancient history right now. His mother was ill and now disaster was closing in on Legend.

He went to his mother and took her by the arm. 'Mother, please be calm, and listen to me. All hell's broken loose down south. I don't know if you're aware of it or not, but Don Mariano has the loco notion we've turned on him and is coming to—'

'At this moment, Chance Stellarman,' Dyana cut in imperiously, 'I'm totally uninterested in whatever drama it is you're talking about. I am only concerned in finding out just how in the name of Heaven a man reputed to be a killer and desperado is wearing the face of a man I once loved.'

Her eyes were clear now, he could see. He was forced to take her seriously.

'Mother, this is all because you have been ill. You allow things that crop up to distress you and—'

'You don't believe what I'm saying, do you?'

'Please, Mother,' Melanie urged, 'Chance only wishes to help. And surely we can discuss this at another time?'

Her face set in determined lines, Dyana whirled and strode to a bureau. She opened a drawer, fanned through a stack of documents, found what she wanted and returned to her son and daughter with a photograph.

'Antonio Villanova!' she said, and held the grainy picture up before Chance's gaze. 'Tell me, do you see any vague similarity between that face and this picture in the newspaper?'

Glancing from one picture to another, Chance felt a chill. For instantly it was apparent the faces of the two handsome young men – the killer and his mother's one-time lover, were virtually identical. Not just similar, but a perfect match in every detail of coloring, expression, bone structure and beauty. It was the quality of uncommon male handsomeness that appeared to be the most overwhelming similarity.

For a long moment of silence, the trouble rapidly closing in on Legend Ranch like a Texas twister seemed secondary. But just what in hell did these pictures signify? Chance asked himself impatiently. OK – so the faces were identical? So? Surely that could only be some weird chance in a million; a trick of capricious fate? What the hell did it matter with the enemy at the gates?

He said as much but Dyana shook her head violently.

'No, far, far more than that, Chance. And now I shall tell you something I never told another soul. When Antonio and my little boy, Ricardo, were supposedly slain by the *Rurales* in Mexico, I knew in my heart that Antonio was indeed dead, but not so my son, despite all evidence to the contrary. That feeling never left me, despite the proof that he was killed when the *Rurales* ambushed Antonio and his banditos, their bodies subsequently destroyed as a warning to other lawbreakers. I always knew in my heart Ricardo lived. And now this picture in the newspaper confirms what I always believed. The man they call Charron is my son – the living image of his father. There can be no other explanation.'

This was too much for Chance right now. He simply couldn't get his brain around this with potential disaster drawing closer by the moment.

Even now, the enemy could be closing in!

He took Dyana by the shoulders and saw her eyes were clear again. Thank God! He needed her right now.

'Palo Pinto, mother. You understand what I've been saying—?'

'Of course, my darling. This is a crisis and we must deal with it.' He was astonished at her total return to normal. Not only had she recovered but was grappling with what was happening and responding to trouble as she always had done – with clear-eyed calm and decisiveness.

She seized his hand and drew him towards the door. 'We must organize the defences and liaise with your father and the boys. We'll send someone out to parley with Mariano, but if that fails, as I suspect it might, then we must prepare for a lengthy siege. Well, what are you waiting for, Chance? There's no time to waste.'

Shaking his head, Chance Stellarman followed his mother's straight-backed figure from the room.

When they had gone, the maid gathered up the pictures they left behind, blinking and frowning as she glanced from one striking face to the other. She

117

had never seen either of the men pictured, but so far as she was concerned, they were one and the same.

Rancho Palo Pinto had become a place of silence and sorrowing women. Joachim dead and Quintaro with him. Now the Don and his two surviving sons storming north with the ranch crew, thirsting for revenge.

The two women took their freshly-cut flowers out to the new graves in the family burial ground by the orchard. An uneasy wind fluttered their skirts and shawls as they came slowly back to the great house. It tugged at their dark mourning dresses and caused them to shield their faces from the flying dust.

It might not seem like the place or the hour when a lady of quality might reach a momentous decision, but such proved to be the case.

When Alma Mariano and her mother entered the vast parlor the mother immediately announced they would leave immediately for Texas and Legend Ranch.

Alma did not comprehend at first; she was still suffering from shock. Eventually her look sharpened however, and she said, 'Mama, what are you saying? We're not going anywhere.'

The mother stared up at a recent oil painting of her handsome husband. The daughter had never seen her look so commanding.

'For all these years I have stood by and watched Sherman Stellarman and your father create pain and misery for themselves and everyone connected to them, simply because Dyana Stellarman long ago chose the Texan to marry and rejected my husband-to-be. I have stood by and watched them jousting with one another ever since and never interfered, believing it was not my place to do so. . . .'

She turned to look at Alma.

'But now my beloved Joachim is dead, and within a week they may all well be dead up there in Texas – Simon, Francisco, your father. Is that why we women keep our silence and allow men to ruin their lives? So they may be spoken of as great ladies who only open their lips to pray for dead sons?'

'What are you trying to say, Mama?'

The wife of Don Miguel lifted her head proudly.

'I have met Dyana Stellarman and consider her a woman of strength and compassion. I believe she must be as opposed to this madness as ourselves.'

She paused to draw breath. When she continued her voice was even stronger than before.

'So, we shall journey to New Mexico and visit with this woman and see if we may stop the madness before all are dead and gone.'

'But, Mama—'

'I will hear no arguments. We shall leave today!'

The first clash between Legend and Palo Pinto took place the following night below Eagle Mesa and across Cripple Creek on the Texas spread's south-western border.

Approaching the mesa warily, the Don's forward scouts were suddenly surprised by cowhands concealed upon a rocky slope.

When called upon to surrender, the Mexicans instead used their spurs and fled. The Stellarman riflemen opened up with a furious volley. Nobody was killed, yet three Mexicans were wounded, two superficially but the third seriously enough to be taken back to Rivertown on the Rio Grande.

Having frittered his chance to surprise, the Don quickly changed tactics. His striking party, with a great display of faked panic, vanished into the timber with plenty of show and noise. Once clear of the battle zone they headed off upstream and were close to the Stellarmans' Five Mile camp come daybreak.

Essential defensive work was still being conducted upon the ranch, for the enemy had arrived far earlier than expected. At the Five Mile, riders with armed escorts were rounding up a sizable bunch of year-lings which needed removing to safer pastures nearer the headquarters.

The Mexicans attacked without warning and the two-hour battle that ensued left three men dead before Chance Stellarman arrived at the head of a bunch of hand-picked cowboys who quickly had the enemy running for cover.

It was a victory of sorts for Legend but this was countered that night when an enemy attack at Black Cow Rock saw Legend forced to retreat and concede several strategic pastures to the enemy.

The enemy was proving far more determined and effective than Sherman Stellarman had anticipated. Forced to take the situation more seriously, Stellarman regrouped his forces at headquarters and dispatched a rider to Longhorn to summon the law.

The rider got through to the telegraph office but help failed to arrive. The sheriff of Danerville had seen too much of the feud over his years in office and wanted no part of it, brushing its aside as yet another manifestation on rich men's excess.

The numbers of wounded arriving at Rivertown increased alarmingly, and when the sheriff finally dispatched two deputies to force a cease fire, both men were wounded and the lawman wired for reinforcements from the Rangers which did not materialize.

Excess had characterized the lives of Stellarman and Mariano and now both arrogant old men were paying the price.

Chance was in the saddle twenty hours a day and fought as hard as any man despite the fact that his heart was not in it. Brother Lafe took a flesh wound and rations were running low at headquarters. But they would never run short of beef, which was just as well, considering his father's total refusal to consider suing for a cease-fire.

That night was strangely quiet on both sides of the river which had become some sort of front line, but first light brought news from Longhorn which would shock Don Mariano and his sons when it reached the lines.

Dona Mariano and her daughter were registered

at the Texas Queen Hotel in Longhorn. They invited Dyana Stellarman to visit them to discuss a matter of 'common interest', as the Dona phrased it.

The matter in question was peace.

CHAPTER 8

ALL THE
PROUD MEN

Two days later found Chance Stellarman standing in a stuffy upstairs suite at the Longhorn Hotel lighting a cigar as he watched two arrogant old men glaring at one another across a crowded center table.

He still could not quite believe it.

Thus far the five-day war which was still sputtering away halfheartedly today just a few miles north, had proven even more vicious and costly than anyone had seemed to anticipate.

And once fully underway, with casualties on both sides mounting by the day, there had seemed no way of either side bringing it to an end with honor until the arrival of the two women now seated with Dyana, Sherman Stellarman and Don Miguel Mariano at the conference table.

He'd been deeply impressed by the intervention of both the woman he loved and her stern-faced mother. Yet with no precedent for such an intrusion in the intermittent wars between the great rancheros over time, to use as reference, he had held out only the slightest hope of success.

Now he sensed he was actually watching it succeed.

Of course, his father and the Don continued glaring and raising points of order in the discussion taking place at the table. But to his experienced eye it was like watching two chained dogs barking furiously while hoping nobody was dumb enough to slip their chains for them.

It was unprecedented, without doubt. Yet effective.

After it was finally over, the two most reluctant men in two nations shook hands under the stern eyes of watchful wives.

The war was over. Yet all that occupied Chance Stellarman's mind as he quit the building later, walking like a weary old man, was the man who had begun it.

No peace in the entire Southwest could be guaranteed while Charron remained at large.

Someone said the killer had been sighted heading for Heartbreak Valley.

The valley was the most hostile stretch of country in the region and the killer headed for it instinctively in the wake of the 'defeat'.

He referred to it as that in his mind even if the Marianos and Stellarmans had struck an honourable truce and quit. His intention had been to shake his pursuers, yet looking back now he could see them still coming, sticking to his trail like so many burrs.

He even knew the hated Canby clan, Dad, Ike and Luke, were tracking for the enemy. There was bad blood with that clan and the killer owed them plenty.

He would be enraged but didn't have the strength for it right now. Or the heart. He could only focus on survival here and now. He would strike back later. He did not accept surrenders or armistices. Death or victory, one or the other.

He reached the far rim of the valley at twilight, paused to roll and light a smoke, looked at the sky, swore at his horse, mounted and rode on into the dusk.

Within the half hour, Chance was standing tall upon the exact spot where the killer had squatted to rest.

He rolled and lighted a durham then went through the routine of seeing to his horse. He sucked smoke deep into his lungs and stared out over the darkening valley, looking as resolute as the statue of a Roman warrior-hero.

He had quit the peace conference with one man to pick up the killer's trail before it got cold, if he could, and had done so.

Several times, his quarry had attempted to outsmart him as they rode the desolate landscape east of Legend. Twice Chance actually feared he'd lost his man, yet had picked up the sign again as though Destiny was at work keeping hunter and hunted linked. At times Chance felt he could figure what his quarry was thinking, and acting upon the hunch, discovered he had been right.

Strange . . . but then they went back a long way together . . . with many a river crossed. . . .

Right now, he sensed his quarry might be beginning to feel just a touch of desperation.

'Chance.'

'Yeah, Blue?'

'There's a camp-fire yonder.'

'Where?'

The man pointed. Chance felt his heart kick when, far out, he spotted a flicker of yellow light at the foot of a gray cliff.

Yet he was wary. Any man who hunted Charron without carefully considering every step he took and every decision he might make, could well be riding on his last manhunt.

'Looks too obvious,' he grunted after a minute. 'Look that way to you?'

'Maybe, maybe not.'

'And that's definite?'

Blue lacked a sense of irony. He didn't smile. 'Well, are we going to take a look?'

'Not right now we're not.'

'You're the boss, Chance.'

'Damn right.'

He was playing this hard. The unexpected intervention of the women into the ever-worsening battle had been a gift, the totally unexpected for which he would long be immensely grateful. But to him, nothing could be finally settled until Charron was finished, either dead or facing justice. He did not intend living the next five, ten or twenty years never knowing from one day to another if he might turn and see him standing on his stoop.

Chance strolled to the edge of the rim rock, trailing tobacco smoke.

The winking red dot of the fire lay about a mile distant across the valley floor. Soon he could make out the silhouette moving about in the fire glow. Every instinct told him it was the killer. He was trying to tempt them to across there. He would never have fallen for that, even before Rinconada, where the killer had reminded him yet again that he was the most dangerous man he'd ever faced.

Chance stood reflecting and enjoying his good cigarette, Then he moved to and fro, watching that distant red dot all the time. When the first stars appeared, he began gathering brush. Within minutes, there were two fires visible in that haunted sector of the valley – one on the valley rim and another on the floor.

He set Blue up as a decoy in his blankets. Then he ate a meal and moved out of the firelight to circle the camp in the darkness.

Throughout the long night that followed he kept circling endlessly, Colt in hand, unlighted cigarette pasted to his lip. Despite the danger, Blue was quickly asleep and snored all night like a buzzsaw.

It was wise of Chance not to do likewise. It was just before first light when a yawning Chance suddenly stiffened at the sounds of a horse, and a ghostly figure appeared.

'Who?' Chance shouted and the moment he failed to get a response he triggered and threw himself full length in the sand.

It was as well he did.

The horse came running into the light with a dummy figure roped to its back. Reacting instinctively, Chance whirled in the opposite direction just as a fast riding figure burst out of the blackness and started in blasting.

Chance rolled desperately, fanning his gun hammer and catching one momentary glimpse of the demonic rider emptying his gun in their direction before the darkness claimed him.

'Did you get him?' Blue shouted, struggling from his blankets.

'Maybe, maybe not. Let's get after him.'

They hunted their quarry throughout the long day. It felt at times they were the only three men on the planet, ducking, weaving, doubling back, playing a game where death might well be the prize.

They lost the killer in the dark hours before moonrise, and it was a weary pair of horsemen who finally were forced to give it best and head back for headquarters.

It was strange to ride into the ranch yard to find the whole place calm and quiet this soon after the violence which had claimed plenty of victims.

They found everyone celebrating the peace but Chance did not join in.

The killer was out there someplace. He could feel him. Maybe he was immortal. . . ?

Only one thing for a man when he began thinking like that. Inside the half-hour he was back in his old comfortable room, fast asleep.

Sherman Stellarman and Don Miguel Mariano stood at opposite ends of the huge stone fireplace in the ranchhouse's enormous west room, vaguely resembling the appearance and attitudes of Ulysses S, Grant and Robert E. Lee at Appomattox Courthouse, if perhaps a shade less friendly.

The warring range lords were here because their women left them with no option. Yet secretly it was exactly what both wanted now. The reality was that both had finally had enough of fighting for life, yet felt obligated to maintain a martial aloofness to the whole matter being dealt with here.

Reflecting his father's manner, Travis Stellarman stood off to one side, sporting a bandaged wrist on one arm, the other arm in a sling. Right now, Travis looked hard and mean in the presence of old enemies, but like the others in the room, was unarmed.

Simon and Franciso Mariano and the wounded Lafe Stellarman all looked very much more at ease. These young men had all done their share of fighting, and had seen far too much of it.

The feud was at an end. Two strong women had decided to end it as they had politely lunched over coffee and cake. The terms they offered their menfolk were strict and hard, and there would be no negotiation. The killing would stop now. Forever. Should it ever be otherwise there would be no wives or daughters to come home to. Ever.

As the documents were signed and smiles finally broke out, Chance felt so relieved, that for the moment at least, he didn't seem to care that Charron seemed to have made good his escape. . . .

While knowing in his heart the man had not been killed. That far from this bright room with its excited voices and hopeful faces, he was still out there.

Somewhere.

CHAPTER 9

FIRE AND HATE

The Canbys were fighting – again.

'I know them's his tracks, old man,' declared rugged Ike, hands on hips and jaw outthrust. 'Know them anyplace. Seems to me any man who can't see that ought rightly to go get his eyes tested.'

That was a bad thing to say. His father was fifty four years of age but still felt twenty five – twenty one on a good day.

'You saying I'm old, mister?' he growled. 'You want me to show you what—'

'For the sweet sake of Judas!' protested the younger brother, rising holding a pot of steaming coffee. 'Will you two get off of it and come chow down before all the sign in Mexico just blows off in the wind?'

Father and son glared at him. But then they caught the whiff of cooking beans and hog ham, and forgot all about who might be old or otherwise.

If the Canbys did one thing better than tracking, it was eating.

The meal over, the man-hunters saddled up and moved on.

Old Dad and big Ike liked nothing better than to get on the trail of some stage bandit or mad dog killer, while a quarry like Charron was about as exciting as things could get.

Ike kept insisting he had the killer's tracks but neither of the others was any too sure. Still, the travelling here was easy, the sign appeared plain enough, and most importantly of all the tracks were leading them back towards their home county, where they just might get to take off some rest time before chasing will-of-the-wisp Charron again.

They were still keenly aware that the killer they dogged now was a far different proposition from the outlaw they'd run to ground before.

They weren't the kind to keep lists or such, but had they done so, Charron would now be top of their danger list.

Over recent months it seemed that killer was intent on striking hard and often. The difficulty was, there never seemed to be a pattern; a tracker could not just sit down, scratch his brain and figure what their quarry might do next. He'd been Number One on various wanted lists both north and south of the border for several months, his reward had shot up, but he was still very much at large.

Dad had promised the sheriff of Tula he would

land the killer before the fall, had been promised double the advertised reward should he fulfil his brag.

Dad had been full of optimism and whiskey the day he'd made that declaration, but felt a long way from being that feisty when they tended their thirst at the long bar in Zuni that night.

For this time they'd really lost the trail . . . whether it had been their quarry's or not.

'Might as well face it,' Lewt stated glumly. 'That son of a bitch is just plain too smart for us.'

That was red rag to a bull. Yet neither father nor brother moved to protest or to clip him in the ear.

What Dad did was take a look at their reflections in the fly-specked bar mirror, and reach a painful decision.

'We're only thirty miles from home,' he said windily. 'We could make it by this time tomorrow night with hard riding. . . .'

'You saying we should quit?' Ike challenged.

'Damn right I am. You want to make something out of that?'

For a long moment, Ike Canby looked as though he might like to do that. Then his hands and thighs began to hurt from too many miles on a horse, and he took a mind-numbing swig straight from the bottle.

'No, damned if I do,' he said after a belch and a scratch. 'Really reckon we could make home by tomorrow night?'

'I don't just reckon,' grinned a revitalised Dad. 'I know!'

*

The dog died without a whimper as the razor-sharp blade whipped across its tautly-held throat.

As hot blood gushed, Charron let the body sag against its chain. He wiped his knife clean on the dead animal's hide and replaced it in its sheath. He liked to be neat. But what he was enjoying even more tonight was the awareness that his slight limp from the injury he'd sustained in Los Santos had finally healed.

As a consequence, he'd found himself easily able to make his way this close to the cabin that had a wide-awake hound dog on watch, reach it without its even sniffing the air in suspicion – then the blade.

He felt stronger, swifter, more confident than ever, which was a fine way to feel on a night and a mission like this.

The sounds of voices and clattering pots and pans washed from the lamp lit windows of the Canby place standing at the foot of Bear Mountain as the silent killer moved lithely across the yard.

He knew that Dad, Ike and Lewt had lived on this remote quarter section for as long as he could recall.

Once or twice over the years he'd come close to paying the sometime manhunters a visit, but this occasion had become more urgent ever since the time the hicks had actually run him down.

He never forgave or forgot.

The sounds of voices and clattering pots and pans washed from the lamp lit windows on the Canby

place as the killer moved silently towards it.]
worked for and with Legend longer than any
the spread, so long it seemed forever. Pop would give
his life for Sherman Stellarman, even now after
Legend had, in his mind, made a huge mistake in
burying the hatchet with the Marianos.

But it was the old bastard's relentless chase after
him that had sealed his fate with Charron. And
tomorrow or the next day a man could guarantee
he'd be out again doing the same thing,

Charron was still faintly surprised at the realiza-
tion he'd waited this long to even scores.

The family was at supper when the shadow fell
across their outside porch. He paused to run a finger
down the woodwork of the kitchen's west wall. He
found the timber totally sun-dried, as expected.

Hunkering down and listening to the clattering
and chattering from within, he drew some notebook
paper from a pants pocket, scrunched it up some,
then wedged it tightly into the crack in the wall he'd
discovered. He quietly scraped a lucifer into life
along the boards and touched it to the tinder. The
little flames that danced were merry and bright as
they briefly lit the killer's flawless features and high-
lighted his big broad smile.

He rose and crossed to the door making no more
sound than a passing shadow.

It was young Lewt who saw him first, due to the
fact that his chair was facing the doorway. He'd never
sighted Charron before but knew him straight off
from the posters and descriptions. But then, who else

135

could it be, strolling into a man's place uninvited right in the middle of one the region's biggest ever manhunts?

The youngest Canby tried to give the alarm, but seemed to be choking on his grub. Ike moved to thump him on the back while the old man growled crankily, just like always.

'How many times does a man have to tell you not to bolt your chow down, damnit?'

But then Lewt pointed, and the two men turned to see the awful danger.

Charron touched his hat and gave a small bow. '*Buenos noches, amigos.* You have had a hard day searching for some filthy *bandido* and have earned an honest meal, no? Well, do not let me stop you. Perhaps I could join you . . . if you would be so kind? Or would it be unfitting for fine Texas gentlemen to sit at the same table as greaser scum?'

The Canbys knew they had to be in the most desperate kind of trouble, even though the killer's hands were empty. It was the intruder's laconic manner and air of total assurance that brought the chill. It shouted a warning to three hard-bitten hunters of bears and men that if they failed to make their play right off, and make it fast, it would be far too late.

Ike's fast right hand dropped below table leather and ripped his Colt .45 from greased leather. Charron's hands blurred, and he began shooting all in one blinding action. Ike Canby was lifted bodily out of his chair by a massive invisible force and hurled backwards with the top of his head missing.

The noise was ear-splitting as the killer's Colts swung on Lewt to storm and storm again.

It was Dad Canby's penance to witness the violent shooting death of both his sons while gnarled old hands, once so supple and swift, appeared to fumble with the .38 thrust in the waistband of his pants.

Gunsmoke was roiling through the room by the time he came clear. He found himself staring into two black gun muzzles, above the six-shooters, a face eager, smiling and excited. It was the worst moment of a hard old man's life, and he knew it had to be the last.

'What kind of low, murdering thing are you?' he managed to get out in a hoarse whisper.

'The winning kind,' Charron laughed.

Gun hammers clicked and two bullets dealt Dad Canby the same swift death he had so often meted out to rustlers who'd violated Legend.

Charron reloaded his shooters and put them away. He helped himself to the barely touched contents of the kid's plate and watched as the hungry flames consumed the porch and began licking through the open doorway.

Servicing his tooth with a pick stick, he strolled on outside, humming some tune.

Now he would concentrate on Legend. . . .

He quit the little valley and rode into the hills at an easy pace, with a freshly lighted cheroot to keep him company. It wasn't long before he glimpsed horsemen pouring down from higher ground to gallop towards the fire.

Wherever he looked, he saw fast-moving horse-men – and dying flames in the night.

The scene reminded him pleasurably of the night he'd ridden from Cibola.

But what had happened in Cibola had been impulsive, unplanned. He'd really taken his sweet time getting round to hard-mouthed old Dad Canby, but it had been well worth the wait, and then some.

He gigged his horse into a trot.

Old Eldio the ferryman sat on an upturned, fish crate and watched the rider swim his horse across the great river.

He switched rheumy eyes to his battered old boat and counted the days since he'd last had a fare. Not many folks travelling these days. All too scared of that damned range war up north. He turned his head and spat. That was his opinion of that sort of caper. They should take a lesson from his book. Eighty years of age and never been in any sort of fight and never would be.

'Hot day,' he remarked as the tall horseman stepped down.

'Aren't they all?'

Chance studied the old river man, wondering why he'd come here today. Certainly Charron's sign had led in this direction, but he didn't expect to find anything here at the ferry crossing. He knew he would not be here but for Dyana. She was still carry-ing on about those pictures, had insisted he forget about hunting Charron and go question the old man instead.

He wouldn't do something like this for anyone but her.

'Drink?' he said, proffering a flask.

The old man's eyes lighted up and he had the bottle uncorked in a twinkling. By the time he'd lowered it, Chance was holding a picture before his face. It was the photograph of the Matador clipped from the newspaper.

'So?' The old man was instantly wary.

'Recognize this man?'

'Everyone knows Charron.'

'But you reared him.'

'Who says?'

'The woman who reckons she could be his mother.'

The ferryman rose to his feet. 'What foolishness do you speak—'

'Listen to me, old man. I don't have much time. I've been checking with river folk on behalf my mother, Mrs Stellarman of Legend Ranch. Since her sighting this picture, which she says is of a son she had here in Mexico at Rosalita some twenty-seven years back, she's been going half out of her mind. She thought her boy was killed when *Rurales* ambushed her outlaw husband and his gang twenty miles into the hills south of here. A child was killed, and she always thought it was her son but never got to see the body. But she has been asking around all over recent, and several folks have told her you reared a kid here years back although you never were married and you never claimed him to be yours. She even gave me a name. Rico.'

'Ahh, Rico . . . the one they now call Matador.'

'Then it's true?'

The old man nodded, lit up a pipe and uncomplainingly proceeded to relate his story with a sad smile. 'I never knew where he came from when he came stumbling from the brush yonder that day, a tiny tyke of about three, beautiful but almost dead from starvation and the buzzards. They had been attacking him but somehow failed to blind him, as they like to do. I had heard nothing of any lost child. So I fed him and he recovered and he stayed with me almost ten years before he left to fight the bulls. . . .'

'Then you are saying that Charron is this boy?'

'That is Rico in that picture . . . and Rico is indeed Charron . . . the greatest sadness of my life that he became as he is. . . .'

Stellarman was stunned by this information. He extracted the second picture which showed the man her mother had run off with in the far past. He'd been astonished when she first showed it to him, for the man in the second photo, Antonio Villanova, the late outlaw, was virtually identical with the killer he'd been hunting!

But if the story was true that a child had been killed in that *Rurale* ambush of the Villanova gang. . . ?

As though reading his thoughts, Old Eldio said, 'Some years after that ambush a man who passed through here told me that a member of that gang whom Villanova met up with that fateful day, had also had a child with him. . . .'

Chance stared. 'Are you saying he might have been the child the *Rurales* burned and buried with the outlaws . . . and my mother's son survived to be reared by you?'

He shrugged.

'Who could be sure? But surely there is no other way to explain the pictures, *hombre.* . . .'

Chance's face was ashen.

'Then I'm hunting my own brother.'

'I loved the boy . . . but as the one who reared him I say to you that the man he has become is no longer a man but a dangerous beast who leaves only the dead in his wake. If you are strong enough and love your fellow man enough, Señor Stellarman, then you must continue to hunt . . . and you must destroy him before. . . .'

His voice choked off.

Chance Stellarman had never heard such fateful words, nor understood any so clearly. He must forget that it now seemed quite probable his mother had given birth to the man known as Charron, the Matador. Forget everything but the fact that should he turn back for the ranch right now he would be responsible for every innocent life the killer might take because he'd failed to do what he knew he must.

'Sorry,' he said, resting a hand on the ferryman's shoulder. 'But you understand. . . .'

The ferryman dabbed at his eyes with a kerchief. 'He was wounded and I dressed his wound . . . he took the trail to Eldio's Peak and beyond. . . .'

CHAPTER 10

SO RUNS
THE RIVER

The old bull ring was still standing. Somehow he knew it would have survived all the years of heat and neglect, the harsh desert winds and the snows of winter, just as it survived the great pestilence that had turned the little village into a ghost town overnight many years ago.

All life had long fled and the desert had encroached between the adobes with sand drifts piled high against the mayor's house where the Matador had once been presented with gifts of gold for his exploits in the ring.

Now he was back, seemingly a thousand years older than that slender, teenage fighter of the bulls who had brought them to their feet screaming his name as he tested and tormented the great beasts before slaughtering them in a way that in itself was a work of art.

He leaned against his weary horse with his head cocked to one side.

He could hear the voices chanting across the years, and they filled him with new strength. He slapped the animal's sweat-streaked neck. 'Go find some grass, muchaha, if there be any left in all the world. . . .'

The animal plodded away and Charron licked dry lips, his frown cutting deep now. Talking to animals. . . ? Had he slipped that far?

Absently he fingered the silver chain encircling his neck. The old man had warned him to not ride too far, but something had driven him to make it all the way to Coronado. For he'd visited here often over the years, as indeed he had other places that meant something to him. He had always had to come. For where others had kin to turn to in times of triumph or disaster . . . Charron had only ever had places.

And this place was clearing his mind and dulling the pain as he moved towards the huge main gates hanging off rusted hinges and creaking in a rising wind.

He had not seen the buzzard.

The devil bird rose with a sudden squawk from a high wooden parapet of the decaying plaza de toros, its crucifix shape with wings outstretched flicking across the hot sand before him as it glided away.

Charron staggered in alarm, momentarily off-balance, unsure for the moment if the scavenger were real or just a fragment of some old dream. And shuddered with his lifetime dread of the ugly ones.

And wondered: could this be an omen?

He blinked and knuckled at his eyes and the bird – if indeed there had been one at all – was gone. It was instinctive for him to rub his shoulders and duck his head as though avoiding cruel beaks and talons. . . .

Yet he felt renewed as he finally squared his shoulders and drew a deep breath into his chest, then strode through the shaded gateway where he had once been adored. And once more heard the rhythm of their chanting: 'Charron! Charron! Charron!'

And understood the reason he had come to this place. To renew, to seek the touchstone of his past, to remind himself what it really meant to be – the Matador!

Proudly he halted, swept off his hat and bowed low . . . as a tiny dot of life appeared to the north where the yellow earth met the sky. . . .

Saddle leather creaked as Chance Stellarman stepped down. His horse was blowing hard and bits of slobber hung from its jaws and the bridle.

It was mid-morning and the day was heating up.

The whole land hummed with small things that buzzed and bumbled in the mounting heat. From the ghost town came the squawk of a buzzard. The bull ring dominated the battered landscape like some long-abandoned castle slowly crumbling into ruin. Clumps of sage thrust slender bayonets of green towards the sun.

He pulled the Winchester from its scabbard and jacked a shell into the chamber. He then looped the horse's reins around a wilting mesquite. Not once did his gaze leave the bullring as he stepped away from his mount to make his way towards the deep gully which the long years had cut close to the huge old building.

There was no sign of Charron or his mount. Yet Chance knew he was here. The sign was plain in the dust, while that faint ticking in his head was like a siren blast warning him the killer knew he was here. Was waiting for him. Smiling, most likely.

Chance's jaw muscles worked as he made his way along the wash in a low crouch. Maybe he was outgunned here, but he would not be easy to kill, not even by a man such as this. He could not let Charron live. It was as simple as that.

The ring loomed closer and taller.

A dust devil danced out of the sagebrush and a tumbleweed came to rest against a sagging gate. Chance came quickly from the gully and immediately squatted low with his rifle, eyes cutting in every direction, every nerve taut. He lifted one hand to massage the knot of tension at the back of his neck.

The sound of the shot came shockingly loud in the hushed stillness, a violent roar of sound which all but drowned the vicious whine of the bullet that whipped over his head and smacked into something hard behind.

He half-rose and touched off three rapid-fire shots in response, then sprang fully erect and darted for the cover of the wall. Two slugs slammed the dry timbers as he took a long slide into cover, but none was close.

He was now close by the northwest main gates. A quick glance revealed a broad expanse of the ring studded with clumps of weed but no sign of his quarry.

'Give up, Charron! You're shooting wild, and I know you've been hurt. You'll be a dead man if you don't quit.'

'I have a better suggestion, Stellarman! Let us both set aside the rifles and step into the open and face one another like men of honor!'

Chance studied the empty terraces before responding.

'You've got no audience here today, killer. You're not wearing your suit of gold with men waiting to cheer when you kill some dumb animal . . . or butcher old men and children like you've done all your life. Give yourself up now before I kill you.'

'I hear fear in your voice, Stellarman!'

Chance had the source of the voice fixed close now.

147

Up swept the Winchester and he pumped two crashing shots into a shadowed doorway.

Instantly Charron's sixgun responded. Chance fired back and glimpsed a figure moving away beyond gapped slats. He sprang to his feet and ran directly for the arena entrance. He was diving headlong for a ticket booth when the lithe figure of his enemy sprang into clear sight a bare fifty yards distant, triggering fast.

A slug clipped Chance's left shoulder and knocked him off balance.

First blood to the killer.

Sprawled behind a bench, Chance set the rifle aside and checked out his Colt .45. He was breathing heavily but there was a great calm growing inside. If he were to die here, he could accept that. He settled down to wait with the patience of an Apache.

The killer also waited. He was arrogantly sure of himself and what the outcome would be, yet just a little less sure than he'd been minutes earlier, maybe just a fraction more respectful of this tall Stellarman whom he'd always recognized as the ace in the Legend deck over the years of blood and death.

He was aware that he'd never before missed a man at such close range.

Before giving that notion time to erode his deadly assurance, the killer forced himself to move. For he was still losing blood and there was no telling how long this hick might wait before making his next move.

He must force the pace.

He cat-footed around the matadors' tunnel then sprinted across a short open space to reach the screened wall directly beneath the president's box.

All senses strained taut, Chance quickly figured out the enemy's new position. He waited a spell, with blood seeping down his arm.

Then he shouted, 'I can out wait you, Charron! Time's on my side here, you son of a bitch, not yours.'

No reply.

Then, a full minute later, a sudden violent crash of gunfire broke the stillness, and Chance was forced to lie flat as snarling lead ripped close, shattering old timbers, wildly ricocheting into the hot sky.

Chance sat breathing deeply, thinking of Alma and his mother to keep calm and controlled, as he knew he must. Then, on impulse, he stripped off boots and hat and clambered atop a water barrel mounted atop the picadors' entrance.

A muffled curse sounded. Reassured that his enemy was still someplace beneath the president's box, Chance moved with infinite caution, placing each footstep with great care as he edged his way along the rotting old roof timbers. Twice he heard a stirring beneath him, twice he paused, listening.

Nothing.

The reason for that was that the killer had managed to wriggle snake-like through the sand until he reached a concealed vantage point where he waited, crouched like a cat, for his enemy to show himself, as he knew he must.

Licking his lips, he told himself he could wait forever if needs be. Chance was their top gun. Kill him and maybe he would feel emboldened to double back on Legend and finish off all the family . . . still mystified why he envied and hated them so much.

The killer was thinking and not listening. When he'd last moved position, the tall man above him had caught a glimpse of shirt sleeve, and using that as a guide, had shifted position with painful care until suddenly he found himself staring directly down at the prone figure ten feet below.

His first thundering shot struck Charron like a thunderbolt and set him rolling violently out into unsheltered space.

Chance triggered again, but fired a fraction too fast.

With lead slashing the dirt beneath his flying feet, the killer was never swifter as he spun away before he could trigger again to dive behind the ancient president's box sturdy side wall.

Launching himself into midair, Chance hit the sand of the ring and deliberately allowed his legs to give way beneath him to cushion the fall. As he hit ground, his enemy bobbed above one of the barricades with gun flame spewing from his hand. The slug ripped a chunk out of Chance's neck yet he made it to his feet, doubled up and darted in pursuit of his man.

For once, Charron's shooting grew wild. Chance should not have made it safely to the deeply recessed doorway of the old infirmary where medicos had once treated the wounded heroes of the plaza de toros, but he did.

Then his legs suddenly gave way. Blood was gushing from his neck. He ripped off his bandanna and applied a tourniquet, every sense alert for the danger that didn't come.

He only realized then, that his silver crucifix on a chain that had been his mother's birth gift to him, was gone. That bullet must have broken the chain.

He should have been outraged but seemed past that point now. Wounded and still leaking crimson, he knew he could afford no more errors. He was weak in the knees as that desert wind now began to blow, peppering sand against the arid walls beyond his safe-hole, then felt uncertainty creep over him.

Suddenly he was overlooking the past and felt an old and bitter fear – the fear that Charron had always been his natural superior; that when the final history of the Stellarman clan was written, it would be seen clearly that not one of them, not his dead brother, the faithful hands or even their legendary gunfighter, Kelso Neils, had ever really stood a chance against this demon from the dry hills of Mexico. . . .

'No!'

He realized he'd said it aloud. Instantly a sixgun

crashed. For a moment he was tempted to return fire before he felt the iron return to his veins. He'd suffered a moment of weakness, but was whole again. He was a Stellarman fighting here for all Stellarman, living and dead.

He would not permit himself to be swept into the dustbin of history by that butcher's guns.

A soft footfall.

Chance lifted his big gun and waited. The killer was very close. He could smell flesh, sweat and leather. What was the bastard waiting for?

Fifteen feet distant, close by the very spot where he had once brought the howling mob to its feet with his matchless grace and courage against the brave bulls, Charron the killer was down on both knees, close to the spot where Stellarman had taken that flesh wound to the throat.

He'd spotted something in the sand, something that appeared familiar. There it was.

Automatically he felt for his neck, thinking his identical cross and chain must have been loose.

It was still in place.

He picked up the crucifix on the bullet-broken chain, the color draining slowly from his face as recognition of the familiar hit hard.

A sense of unreality gripped the gunman as he turned the cross over and saw the inscription on the back: 'To my dearest son.'

His mind reeled. It was incomprehensible that Stellarman the blood enemy should possess such a thing. An identical replica with the exact same inscription as the one he had worn round his neck all his life?

Then he realized that this could only be some low and evil Stellarman ruse or trick intended to trick or confuse him. The *bastardo!*

A red film of rage clouded his vision . . . then the blinding flash of total hatred. The sixgun in his fist began to tremble. He lusted to kill far more intensely than ever in his murderous life.

He sensed Stellarman was wounded, perhaps badly, and maybe lying helpless just waiting to be put out of his misery.

Charron knew that, sick or well, he had the guts to finish the bastard off. Yet even with the thought came the other; first he must know about the crucifix, not simply be satisfied with a guess.

He moved laterally to bring the infirmary door into sight. He could hear the wounded Stellarman's heavy breathing. Cupping the crucifix and chain in his hand, he tossed it to land within the infirmary where it lay glinting upon the sand covered floor.

'You will explain this, gringo scum!' he snarled, fury dominating him. 'What filthy trick is this?'

'What trick, butcher?' Chance made his voice sound strong.

'On the back. That trick! How did you know?'

No answer.

Chance had picked up the cross and chain, feeling his scalp pull tight.

'Where did you get this, Stellarman?'

'I've had it all my life! Where did you get yours from?'

'You lie in your stinking teeth.'

It was in Charron at that moment to risk leaping from cover and just blasting, so intense was his anger and confusion. And yet he could not . . . not without understanding this mystery.

'I have always had it,' he panted. 'It is mine. I was wearing it when . . . when it happened. When the buzzards came after me . . .' He was forced to break off and loosen his collar as emotions gripped like steel. 'When . . . when I was running from the guns and ran and ran until I came to the great river where the old man saved me from . . . from the devil birds. . . .

It was silent for a long moment.

Then, 'Well, gringo scum?'

Chance felt light-headed as he leaned back with the cross still in his hand. What the killer said . . . his description of 'running from the guns' and the position of Old Eldio's riverside place in relationship to the region where his mother's lover had been slaughtered that day long ago . . . all conjured up a scenario he could scarce deny.

It could have happened.

Charron, the child, could have survived and fled that terrible day – he already knew from Eldio that another child had apparently been found among the *Rurales'* victims that day. Eldio . . . had taken him in, reared him, lost him when he went off to fight bulls and eventually to strap on the guns he'd never since taken off. . . .

'No, it can't be,' he groaned aloud.

'What?' Only curiosity stronger than life itself was holding the killer back. He had to know. 'Tell me what it means, Stellarman, I have to know.'

Chance told him.

It was silent as the grave save for the hiss of whispering sand after Chance fell silent. Then a voice scarcely recognizable as Charron's reached him faintly.

'My mother . . . your mother? It must be. And to think I may well have killed her when we attacked the rancho . . . killed all of you . . . half brothers and sister . . . if all this is true. But surely it can not. . . ?'

His voice trailed away.

'Killer?'

'What?'

'Think on this. If this is true what we think . . . and I reckon it is, then you ought to know that mother always believed you were alive, and always loved you.'

He heard a rustling. The sun filtering through fogging sand cast a shadow in the doorway. Chance clutched his Colt tightly, ready to fight to the death.

'Loved me?'

Chance risked a quick glance round the door-jamb. The killer stood there with six-shooter in either hand, blinking and swaying. His lips moved. Chance took a fresh grip on his gun handle.

There appeared on the killer's face such a look of naked emotion that Chance was almost forced to look away. But when he saw tears coursing down that pale and handsome face, he felt his resolve weaken and was about to speak when the madness and hatred returned. He saw it happen, and it happened in one moment out of time. There was the cruel twist of the mouth, the flaring eyes, the suspicion, hate and savagery of a lifetime flooding back following one moment of weakness.

As those big guns came jerking upwards.

'Lying, stinking gringo scum!'

Charron had returned to type and murder blazed in his eyes as he triggered. But the killer could not see straight for the tears in his eyes. Chance could. He fired two bullets at point blank range and the killer was going down, striking the earth with one shoulder, rolling to face the arena where he had once been king.

Chance moved through the gunsmoke and dropped on one knee at the killer's side. Charron's eyes flickered and he coughed, a trickle of crimson at the corner of his mouth.

He spoke with great effort.

'Brother, don't let the buzzards find me,' he whispered.

Chance brushed the hair from his forehead and held him tightly against his chest until he died.

'Someone comes, Grampa.'

'Who? Someone to be taken across the river?'

'Just one man, Grampa. A gringo.'

Old Eldio squinted against the glare to see the tall rider guide his horse across the river sand. He recognized him then. He was both wary and curious as he spoke.

'So, I see you survived, Señor Stellarman.'

Chance did not reply immediately. He was staring across the great river that had flown forever through Indian history. In the far distance stood One-Tree Hill which marked the southern boundary of the Legend.

The scene was peaceful. The old man continued to stare up at him questioningly.

Chance thrust a hand into his pocket and brought out the cross and chain, holding it up.

The old man appeared to sag a little, then straightened and rose from his stool.

'Better this way, I suppose, Señor. As we all know, he grew to be a wicked man who—'

'No. He was my brother.'

Old Eldio stared, not understanding. Nor did he seem to understand when the horseman made a small ball of crucifix and chain and hurled it far across the river where it vanished with a small plop of sound.

'*Adios*, brother,' Stellarman said. 'And adios to you, old man. That's a fine grandson you have there. I'd have high hopes for him if I were you.'

He turned the horse and was soon breasting the fast flowing waters. Man and boy stood watching his figure recede.

'What did he mean about his brother, Papa?'

'I know not.'

'But you know all things.'

Old Eldio shook his head, watching the streaming horse emerge on the northern side of the river.

'Only the great river knows all things, my boy. Only the great river.'